CADAVER ON CANAL STREET

PARANORMAL WOMEN'S FICTION: TWISTED SISTERS
MIDLIFE MAELSTROM BOOK 2

BRENDA TRIM

"The only person you are destined to become is the person you decide to be."

CHAPTER 1

*D*anielle

THERE WAS an undeniable pep in my step as Lia and I walked down Canal Street. We were meeting with a new client that wanted us to throw her a birthday party. It was the siren Noah and Lucas had referred our way.

It was less than two months ago since Phoebe had released the magic in the plantation's land that my sisters and I had purchased as a venue for our party planning business. She awakened our magical heritage in the process and life hadn't been the same since then.

Initially, I'd worried I had made a mistake in pushing my sisters to invest in the rundown antebellum mansion and grounds. When the first ghost appeared, a leaky roof and a ghoul quickly followed, convincing me that we were doomed. It didn't take long to change that opinion.

Two sexy shifters came to our rescue, fixed our roofs, and became our first clients to book an event at Willowberry. Six

Twisted Sisters still had existing parties booked, but none were at our venue. The mortgage on the place necessitated continued bookings which meant we couldn't turn down anyone wanting a party. Hence the reason we were walking around the French Quarter less than a week after Mardi Gras.

"God bless it, this place is a zoo." Lia was right about that. It was like watching a pinball game with drunk people stumbling down the sidewalk clutching their vividly colored cocktails. And it would only get worse after night fell.

"The hassle will be worth it. A siren asked us to throw a party for her. I wonder if she knows any mermaids." I didn't bother to hide what I was saying. New Orleans was known for its supernatural connections.

Mermaids and sirens sounded better than necromancers and voodoo gods. I hoped we wouldn't see Marie Laveau again anytime soon. She had tried to hijack the ritual to give our ghoul a soul.

When Phoebe had first brought Camilla back, I thought she was a zombie. She looked and acted like one when she first materialized by the beehives at the plantation. Discovering a ghoul was nothing like a zombie was one of the first lessons we'd learned since being thrown in the deep end of the magical world.

Talk about trial by fire. Good thing I used to be on the transport team for the NICU department at the hospital. There you had to roll with it and learn as you went.

"We have our second client, so it already is worth it. What was the name of the bar, again?" Dahlia tucked her white-blonde hair behind one ear as she scanned the area.

"It's called Final Swallow. It's on Royal Street." I'd never seen or heard of it.

There were more bars in the French Quarter than there were ghosts and vampires. At least I hoped that was true. I honestly had no idea. It was something we grew up saying. Now, I wondered how accurate the claim was. I'd have to ask Noah.

Just thinking the sexy shifter's name made my thoughts turn gooey. It stunned me that he'd worked his way past the house of ice surrounding my heart. After two shitty marriages, I'd sworn off men and was focusing on myself.

That lasted all of two minutes. The first hot guy to bat his lashes at you and you caved. Sometimes, I hated my inner snark. She could be a real bitch.

Dahlia laughed and for a second, I thought I'd said that out loud. "A guy named that place. No way would a woman have anything to do with that double entendre. Still, they must have some potent stuff in the place."

I rolled my eyes at my sister, but couldn't stop the laughter. It died quickly when something occurred to me. "It's not a strip club, is it? I will kill Noah if he has sent us to a titty bar." There were clubs where men and women took off their clothes throughout the Quarter, so it was possible.

Lia threw her hands in the air and shook her head. "How the hell should I know? What's the address? Royal isn't that big, and we've been on it for a few blocks."

I stopped and pulled my phone out. The device unlocked with facial recognition, but I couldn't press any of the buttons with my gloves on. I'd taken to wearing them all the time since my psychometry had emerged, to avoid having visions of the past.

It was especially bad in the house. The third time I saw a slave get beaten, I was over the appeal of a plantation house. There were plenty of good times as well. But being thrust into the past took a toll on me, which was why Lia had ordered me the supple, black, leather gloves. They were supposed to be touchscreen capable. That worked as well as my Uncle Rob, and he has never worked a day in his life.

Lia held out her hand. "Here, give me that."

I handed her the phone. It wasn't until her eyes widened I realized she would see the previous message from Noah. "Wait, I'll get it."

"Nuh-uh. This is some juicy stuff. He wants to take you to dinner and show you how a goddess should be worshipped. Damn, sis, that sounds hot. At least he knows you're better than the average woman and deserves to be treated like royalty."

Heat scalded my cheeks, and I wanted to crawl into a hole. I was afraid my sisters would think I was moving too fast. They were too nice to say anything to me, but they would think it.

"Shut up. He's trying to woo me. Of course, he's going to say stuff like that. It means nothing." I snatched my phone and looked at the address while not really seeing it.

Lia put her hands on my shoulders and made me focus on her. "That's not true and you know it. Neither Noah nor Lucas are the type of guy to snow a woman. They don't have to say that to get laid. They're gorgeous, with bodies of Greek gods. Noah really likes you. Anyone can see it in the way he looks at you. I know you're nervous after what you've been through, but you don't have to worry about this. Be open to possibility and let it happen naturally."

I sighed and nodded my head. "I'm going to need you to remind me of that a hundred more times. Let's get to the Final Swallow." I scanned the number of the business behind us. "Looks like we passed it already."

Dahlia let the topic go. It was why she and I could live with one another without coming to blows. She would never push me to talk about more than I wanted to. "That's odd. I didn't see it."

We turned back the way we'd come and were both looking at the addresses and names on storefronts. When we reached the address, I understood why we had passed it. It was located in a courtyard hidden by a hedge.

"It's in there." I pointed to the space behind the hedge. It was fine now, but I imagined it would be scary at night with nothing more than a gas lantern to light your way.

New Orleans, and the French Quarter, in particular, were known for their courtyards. Most had cafes or small shops inside them. It was one of my favorite things about the area, aside from the Creole architecture. It provided privacy while still being in the middle of the hustle and bustle.

Dahlia walked through the space behind the hedge, and I followed suit. The cement sidewalk gave way to a tiled patio that had a fountain as big as one of ours in the center. The surrounding building was two stories high, and the stucco was painted a terracotta color. There were plants and trees everywhere. It was like walking into a paradise.

"It's in the corner there. It appears to be the only business here," I pointed out.

I stuck close to Dahlia as she opened the wood door. The bar was vastly different from the beautiful courtyard outside. Bartender aside, it looked like any bar I'd ever been inside. It was dimly lit with dark walls. There were tall bar tables with bar stools closest to the long wooden bar. Bottles of alcohol stood at the ready in rows on shelves.

My gaze got stuck on the thing making the drinks. The devil was indeed in New Orleans and working at Final Swallow. The spade-tipped red tail waved over the creature's shoulder. As if it had felt my stare, its black eyes focused on me, making me shiver.

"What can I get you, beautiful ladies?" The voice was deep, indicating it was a guy. He tilted his head, and I followed the movement of his red horns.

Lia cleared her throat. "Um, we're here to meet with Nedasea. We're from the Six Twisted Sisters."

"You must be Danielle and Dahlia," a beautiful woman called out. It was the only thing that broke my gaze from the red-skinned demonic creature behind the bar. "Thank you for coming. I was so excited to hear about you guys. This birthday is particularly important for me and I wanted a big bash to mark the occasion, but I don't have the time or talent to make it what I really want."

I snapped out of my daze and plastered a smile on my face. "That's what we do best."

Nedasea tossed long teal hair over her shoulder and cocked a hip. "Before we get started, do you guys want Brezok to make you anything to drink?"

"I'd love a pina-rita if it's not too much to ask." Lia took a seat at the empty table closest to Nedasea.

Brezok picked up a bottle without looking and tossed it in the air. "That's easy enough. I prefer tequila over rum, too."

Lia laughed. "It's not the tequila really, but the combination of lime juice, pineapple, and coconut that I'm addicted to."

Seeing Dahlia at ease helped me loosen up and forget about the demon serving us drinks. I sat next to her and ordered the same thing. I took a moment to look around the bar and noticed there was no stage for a band or dance floor. The place was filled with tables, most were wood and had seating for four people. The place had more customers than I expected.

Nedasea sat down with the drinks and rubbed her hands together. "Alright, here's what I'm thinking. I'd like to do an underwater theme. Can you guys get some big shells and starfish? How about a boat? Oh, do you have a pool?"

I laughed at her enthusiasm. It was infectious, and my mind immediately started churning through various ideas. "We don't have a pool, but we do have several large ornamental fountains. And the perfect location for your underwater theme. It's outside, so your guests can enjoy the fountains and garden."

"It's also shielded in the event of rain. It's between the main house and the large kitchen your caterers can use," Lia added.

Nedasea's face fell. "You don't do the food?" There was a quality to her voice that made the back of my neck prickle. It highlighted that I really knew next to nothing about her kind.

I immediately wondered if the myths were true about sirens luring men to their deaths. Could she enthrall us with her voice? Or would she eat us for dinner? Each thought was more ludicrous than the last. I wanted to ask the questions racing through my head but didn't dare.

I shook my head. "We focus on the decorations and creating precisely what you want. However, we work with many restaurants and can arrange the food. All you need to tell us is what you want to serve and your budget, and we will make it happen."

The siren was back to clapping her hands. "That's wonderful. Now about the decorations. Do you think we can get a giant conch shell? And make it sparkle? They've been my favorite since I was a girl."

Dahlia set her glass down. "As long as you are okay with it not being the real thing, we can do that. We have two options. We can use our CNC machine to engrave it in an inch thick piece of plywood, or I can cut one out on our laser out of quarter-inch birch. We would paint either and use glitter."

"What's the difference? I don't know what either of those things is or how it would look."

"Neither would be a true shell. Both would be flat-backed. The one done on the CNC machine would be heavier and we can engrave ridges into it. The laser would be layered wood and have a slightly different look and be thinner. I'll make some small ones and we can get together another time and I can show you what they look like."

Nedasea was all smiles. "That's perfect. Oh, I can't wait. I want this to be perfect. Elegant and fun. Wait, what about alcohol? Are we allowed to serve it on the plantation?"

Her question caught me mid-sip. My eyes widened, and I made a noise of appreciation. Demon or not, Brezok could make a mean drink. Speaking of, she'd asked about serving alcohol at her party. "We can't serve the drinks, but we can hire a bartender that comes with a license and insurance to do it for us. That covers the requirements and allows you to have alcohol."

Lia sat forward and clasped her hands around the stem of her glass. "One thing we have to consider is that we don't know any paranormal bartenders. All of our contacts are of the mundane variety."

Nedasea cocked her head and looked between us. "How do two witches who have a party business only deal with mundies? And not have paranormal vendors?"

I sighed. This was a long story, and I didn't want to get into it with the siren. It showed our vulnerability. There were too many in this room that could use it against us. "Most of our clients are mundies. However, we have been looking for a reliable magical resource. I have a call with Kaitlyn later to see if any of her witches are bonded and licensed."

"I'm available," Brezok called out across the bar. "I can have one of my employees fill in for me."

Nedasea rolled her eyes and scowled at the demon. "You just want to come and feed off the attention you'll get. There's a reason I haven't invited you, Brezok."

"I'll order extra Highland Park and be there early so I can

set up my bar." The demon didn't seem to hear Nedasea say no to him.

To my surprise, she winked at me with a smile, then sighed like she was put out. "You'd better be on your best behavior. No preening on my birthday, dammit."

Lia looked at the bartender. "What do you mean by feeding on attention?"

Nedasea furrowed her brow and opened her mouth, but Brezok cut her off. "I'm a fame demon. I survive by being a household name. Most of my kind wear glamors to look like mundies and work in Hollywood. It's a cop-out if you ask me. They don't have to work for their survival. It isn't hard to hide behind a pretty façade."

Nedasea laughed. "You're so full of shit, Brez. You never learned to cast an effective glamor. That's why you own a bar and feed from scraps."

We discussed budget, food choices, and the number of guests she expected for the next half hour. It didn't take long to get comfortable with the fame demon and Nedasea. She knew what she wanted, which made it so much easier for me. We exchanged information with Brezok and came up with a tentaive agreement for him to work with us.

I stood and smiled at the siren. "We will be in touch. If you have questions or want to share other ideas, you both have our numbers."

Nedasea smiled and pulled me into a hug, then Dahlia. "I do. You guys are so easy to work with. I can't wait to see the samples."

We took our leave, I was grinning from ear to ear as we made it to Royal Street. "We sounded like professionals in there. Even with a demon manning the bar and giving us his number, that was less stressful than working in the NICU."

Lia bumped my shoulder as we walked. "We've been professionals since the very first party we threw. You have an amazing ability to come up with a hundred little things that show the clients we pay attention to every small detail. That's something I couldn't do with decades of training."

I chuckled at my sister's comment. She didn't give herself enough credit. "You are more talented than you know, sis. You are the one that creates everything on the laser and CNC machine. None of us could do that."

Lia snorted. "I can only do that because you tell me what we are putting together. I'm a proud worker bee. I'm pretty excited about coming up with some designs for a conch shell. That's one we haven't done yet."

I had an idea of how we can add that to the centerpieces. "I was thinking we could use the rustic metal lanterns with driftwood and we could cut out conch shells on the laser to include in a floral bouquet."

Lia shook her head. "See, that right there is why you're queen bee. Phi comes in as a close second. Kota, too. We have to use holographic glitter on them."

"What do you think about having the demon be a bartender?" I ignored the tourist that looked at me funny.

Dahlia turned left onto Canal and smiled sweetly as we left the guy staring at us. "It's not like we have a choice. We can't take the chance that all of her guests will look entirely normal. The last thing we need is for someone to go screaming all over New Orleans that we are a bunch of freaks. It's unlikely most would believe what they were seeing. Humans have a way of explaining away things that make them uncomfortable. Still, I don't want to deal with that. I liked your idea of asking Kaitlyn, though. We should do that regardless so we can find one for next time."

"I don't know. Brezok would likely be happy to become our de facto bartender. I bet the attention he gets at the bar has greatly diminished, given that he's so commonplace there."

I stopped when I realized Dahlia wasn't with me. Turning, I lunged when her knees gave out and she collapsed. Shit, shit, shit! She was having a vision. Now plenty of people stopped and were staring at us.

I held her close and jostled her. "Dahlia. Are you okay?" I kept my tone moderate, not wanting to alarm any of the bystanders.

"Do you need help? I can call an ambulance," a young woman about my oldest daughter's age asked me.

I shook my head, hoping she didn't see the sweat rolling down my temples. "My sister had minor surgery not too long ago, and she's overdone it. She's going to be alright. Thank you, though."

I said a silent prayer that Dahlia snapped out of it so we could get the hell out of there. We were drawing attention that I'd much rather avoid.

CHAPTER 2

*D*ahlia

Anyone that spent time in the French Quarter knew they'd be surrounded by stale alcohol, sweat, urine, and vomit. It was a unique sludge created by countless tourists drinking and not making it to the bathroom for any purpose.

Dani and I had been walking along, and I was fine until a sweet scent joined the mix. It was a cross between flowers and citrus. I'd become accustomed to the sensation of a smell consuming my entire focus.

I stopped immediately and stiffened my legs so I didn't faceplant on the cement while the vision overtook me. The world wavered and dizziness sent me to my knees. So much for staying upright. My jaw clenched in anticipation of breaking a knee cap. There was nothing I could do to slow my descent.

A soft, warm body caught me. I hoped to God it was Dani because it would be awkward if it were a stranger. I couldn't tell who it was because my vision had blurred and the current people walking down Canal disappeared. My heart raced as I looked around.

The noonday sun was replaced by stars and the moon. There were few people milling about, so it must be after two in the morning. As a popular destination, the French Quarter had people walking around all night and day. That number decreased drastically when they staggered to their rooms and passed out for the day.

I watched several cars drive past after the only couple on Canal entered the hotel next to me. It was one of the chains, not a boutique hotel like we were known for. The sound of an engine was loud in the quiet night.

My head swam as I turned to see who it was. What I saw stopped my heart. There was a big guy with broad shoulders dressed in black and he was putting a woman down on the sidewalk, leaning her against the hotel.

Either she brushed her sandy brown hair with egg beaters or she's had a rough night. It was in knots and there were leaves and sticks in it. She was wearing a pink top that was skewed and torn jeans. She'd look like one of the homeless that lived on Canal if her clothes weren't so clean.

I was so focused on her, that I didn't see the guy leave. Something wasn't right with this vision and it had to do with her. My heart was in my throat as her head lolled in an unnatural angle.

The breeze blew her hair away from her forehead, and I gasped when I saw her vacant stare. I couldn't tell precisely what color her eyes had been because they'd taken on the gray hue after death.

I was staring at a cadaver on Canal Street, knowing this woman was very likely still alive at that moment. You see, my visions are of the future, so this hasn't happened yet. My head snapped up, and I scanned the street, trying to find the car or the guy. I needed to know more information.

My neck whipped back and forth like I was a bobblehead doll and between one blink and the next, I was staring at pinched brown eyes. Dani sighed heavily. "Lia, thank God. Are you alright?"

The feel of being watched made the hairs on the back of my neck stand on end. Was the killer around us right now? No, but a dozen tourists had stopped and were watching us like we were Thursday night's dramas.

"I'm okay. Just got a little woozy. Nothing to worry about."

Dani nodded. "I told you we shouldn't overdo it." Deciding we were as fun to watch as paint dry, the crowd dispersed slowly.

Dani tried to haul me away as well, but I resisted. Five feet from me was the exact spot where the woman would be dumped by her killer. There was a stain on the side of the building that was driven into my grey matter like a spike. I'd never forget this spot or what was going to happen here.

"What are you doing? We need to get the hell out of here before you have another episode." Dani was wrong. Finding the woman before she was killed was exactly what I needed to do.

To say Dani was stressed was an understatement. Her voice couldn't get any more strained. Not that I blamed her. It had been less than a couple of months since our magic was awakened like the anciek kraken. From the moment Phoebe had released it, tentacles of power had permeated my body. I used to wish for more exciting powers.

I kept trying to shoot fire from my hands or make rainfall with a command, but nothing happened. Whoever decided my fate knew what they were doing because if I could have done those things too, we'd have a flood rolling down Canal while the hotel burned to the ground. That vision had shaken me like a dry martini.

"We can't leave yet. I need to try and make another one

come. If I don't get more information, a woman will be killed and dumped right here."

Dani's gasp could be heard in the bayou, so I was surprised none of the gawkers came back to see what was happening now. *You two are as exciting as watching water boil. No one wants to stick around for that.* My snarky side had a point there.

"What? Are you serious? Don't answer that. Of course, you're serious. How the hell are you going to make yourself have another vision? Your smell-o-vision is less predictable than Dakota's period right now."

I wrinkled my nose at Dani's description. I didn't want to think of Kota's irregular menstrual cycle. It made me think about what awaited me right before I hit menopause. The night sweats had just started for me, and were currently few and far between. I couldn't imagine becoming the swamp thing nightly, while never knowing when I'd start bleeding or how bad it would be.

I took a deep breath, hoping to catch the scent again. When the usual toilet bowl didn't tickle my fancy, I shrugged my shoulders. "I have to at least try, sis. I can't walk away and ignore what I just saw. Please."

Dani winced and gestured back the way we'd come. "We might as well retrace our steps and see what happens, but stick close to me. I'm a runner, but not a weight lifter. I'd rather you slump against me than I have to catch you, again. I think I pulled a muscle just now."

I winced. Dani had been at my side through some of my worst moments and still was. She even gave up her honeymoon to come and be with me after Leo died. I was in a bad place then and my kids surely would have died if she hadn't shown up with her new husband and helped me grieve and work through the worst of the loss.

"It was probably those toffee peanuts I can't seem to

resist. They've added ten pounds." Alright, so it was closer to fifteen, but who was counting? Not me. I'd never eat those nuggets of deliciousness again if I did.

"Between the two of us, we could lose a small child if we could give up our vices. Sadly, the Tall Boys call to me as often as the nuts do you. Speaking of drinks, I could use a Pepsi. I think there's a place on Decatur that has it on tap."

I slowed when we reached the spot I had the first vision. "It's that taco shack, isn't it?"

She nodded as I sniffed the air like a bloodhound seeking a trail. A shiver raced through me when I realized how accurate that description was. I saw a dead woman. I was a social worker by trade and had clients that died, but I wasn't like Dani, who had seen many of her patients pass away.

"Let's keep walking. I'm not getting anything yet. This magic shit should come with a handbook. Do you think mom knew we had witches and Fae in our lineage?" I highly doubted she had known with certainty. But I wonder if she sensed something.

Dani took her job of sticking close, literally. She was glued to my side and even threaded her arm through mine. "I'm not sure. It's possible. She was always drawn to para-normal shows and books. And she swore she could see ghosts, Deandra too. Remember when we teased her about seeing the woman in the pink floppy hat and mom made us stop? Whether or not she knew we had it in our blood, she believed in the supernatural."

"That's what I was just thinking. If she had been with us when Phoebe unlocked us, she'd have taken to her powers like a duck to water. Sometimes I wonder why I didn't inherit her ability to master things."

Dani chuckled and shook her head as she turned down Decatur. "We got some of it, but dad's genes come into play with us too, so we aren't as adept or confident as she was. I've never seen anyone use a scroll saw the way she could."

"That's why I purchased the laser and the CNC. They're much easier. I don't have to have a steady hand." That was my problem. Anytime I tried to cut something as simple as a circle, it looked like a toddler threw a tantrum while holding a power tool.

"Those were the best purchases next to Willowberry. I love how the plantation is coming along. The planter boxes near the kitchen turned out stunning." She entered the restaurant as we reached it.

Following her inside, I inhaled the spicy, cumin scent of the Mexican food. It was such a stark contrast to the street that I worried I would be pulled into another vision. My stomach grumbled and my mouth watered and I was not sucked into scenes from the future.

"Wanna get some tacos?"

Dani looked over her shoulder at me and laughed. "Silly sestra. Like we would leave without a couple of carne asada street tacos."

I chuckled, and we placed an order, then went to fill our cups with drinks. Our order was ready a minute later and we left, heading back toward the hotel where I'd seen the dead woman.

"Grab one and eat it before they get cold." Dani held out the bag filled with foil-wrapped packages.

My hand was halfway inside the bag when I pulled it away empty. "Nah, I'll wait. The smell will throw me off."

Dani shrugged and unwrapped the top half of a taco and ate while we walked. The street was less crowded this time, making me hope it wasn't a combination of body sweat that had triggered it last time.

A cold wind blew in from the river, making me shiver. I was about to give up when the sweet smell combined with a frat house hit me again. I sucked in my breath as the world wavered and my knees gave out. My soda dropped from my fingers and splashed on the sidewalk.

Day became night, and the people disappeared. I didn't think about anything except finding the woman. To my surprise, she was already against the building. Her head was in the same position.

My horror was shoved aside so I could move past her face. When my gaze landed on her chest, my stomach roiled and bile used my tonsils as punching bags. Her chest was slashed open, and she was covered in blood and viscera.

Through stinging eyes, I was able to make out four long gashes that had definitely been the cause of her death. White shone through the red along with dark maroon. *Organs and bone.*

This vision didn't last nearly as long. I was yanked back to the present with wet shoes, smashed against my sister's boobs for the second time that hour. I groaned and balanced on my feet.

Dani scowled at me. "That's it. We're leaving now. You need to rest."

I was missing my audience this time, so escape was easy. I snatched my empty paper cup from the ground and followed Dani. "Did anyone see that time?"

"Thankfully, you weren't out that long. One guy cursed at you for splashing his sneakers while another lady laughed at you."

People were assholes sometimes. "Humanity astounds me."

Dani snorted. "If I'd seen it, I would have laughed too. You looked like you'd had one too many yards and could no longer walk straight. So basically, you fit right in down here."

I tossed the cup in the trash and wrapped my coat tighter. February in New Orleans wasn't like it was in Chicago, but it was cold for us. Especially when you were close to the water. *Or just saw a woman that was clawed to death lying there on the sidewalk.*

Dani offered me a taco, but I shook my head rapidly from side to side. "No thanks. I lost my appetite. I don't think I will ever eat again."

Dani shot me a concerned look. "Was it worse than before?"

I inclined my head. "Let's just say I need to have a conversation with Lucas and Noah about the guys they stopped on our property. I want to make sure none of them continued their crime spree."

Dani dropped the rest of her taco into the sack and took a sip of her drink. "I almost hate to ask, but what do you mean? Did you see them?"

I shook my head. "I didn't see anyone except her this time. The first time I saw the back of the guy that dumped her, but not his face or car. I know it needed a new muffler because it was loud. The claw marks were unmistakable. I'll never be able to forget them."

Dani squeezed my hand. "I've seen some awful injuries, so I can imagine. Maybe we can narrow it down. What was the weather like? Can you tell those things in your visions?"

I considered her question for a few seconds as we reached the car and got inside. "I honestly don't know. I was so shocked this time. When it happened before, I was too new to really analyze the experience. I can tell you it was likely after two in the morning, otherwise I can't say much else."

Dani sighed as she backed out of the spot and pulled onto the street. "Perhaps we should go to the police and let them know."

I scoffed and gaped at my sister. "And say what? That I have visions of the future that are triggered by strong smells and I saw a guy dump a cadaver on Canal Street? Yeah, that'll go over well. I'm sure they will be grateful and stake the site out until they come across the culprit with the woman who lost her life. Because I have nothing that will lead them to the killer or the victim. Not to mention that they will lock me in the looney bin for sure."

Dani held up a hand. "Alright, I get your point. It was a stupid suggestion. I don't see how there's anything we can do. We have no information to go on and we have no idea who we are trying to save."

A rock settled in my gut with her words. She was right, but I couldn't give up and ignore it completely. "We might not have any information, but we know a location and the fact that a shifter is likely responsible. There has to be a connection to the dumpsite. I can't sit by and do nothing. She's alive right now, but she might not be for long."

Dani sighed. "We will talk with the others and see if they have any suggestions."

I rubbed one temple while leaning my head against the window. I was exhausted after having back-to-back visions. I could use a nap. However, I doubted I would be sleeping anytime soon, given that the image of the dead woman was haunting me.

CHAPTER 3

*D*anielle

I watched Dahlia as she stood at the stove making etouffee with Camilla for dinner. She enjoyed cooking far more than I did, for which I was grateful. We needed someone to feed us. Cami had done a good job of it for the past few weeks. I suspected Lia felt guilty about that and had chosen this moment to learn and help as a way to distract herself.

This wasn't the worst I'd seen her. That had to be the time right after Leo died, but this was a close second. Lia had a big heart and wanted to help everyone. It's what made her a good social worker for two decades.

"Smells good, sestra. Whatcha making?" Dakota breezed into the kitchen in the main house, with Dreya right behind her.

Lia turned from the stove. "We're making crawfish etouffee and bean burritos for Dani."

My heart squeezed at how my sisters always thought of me and my quirks. I had the palate of a teenager. "Thanks,

Lia. I appreciate that. I will try the dish, though." I might have unrefined and picky tastes, but I try everything.

"You'll love this one. It's so yummy. I hope it's one of Cami's recipes," Dre added.

Dahlia beamed at Camilla, making me hope she was getting back to normal. "It is one of hers."

Dakota cooked often for her family and was good with all sorts of recipes, so I wasn't surprised when she joined Lia at the stove. "Is it very different from what you usually make?"

Lia shrugged her shoulders. "So far the differences are minor."

"But the flavor will be unlike anything you have ever tasted," Camilla promised. "This recipe was taught to me by my father and his mother in your house, Dreya."

It was easy to forget Cami was a resurrected slave that had lived hundreds of years ago. The history of her area was rich and diverse and a lot of it wasn't talked about often. Slavery on the plantations was one of the black spots in our past, if you asked me. I'd seen enough of how Camilla and the others were treated to know we couldn't begin to comprehend how bad it was for them.

Dre grabbed a tea from the fridge. "Are there any recipe books hidden under the floors? I'd love to learn more."

Camilla shook her head from side to side. "Everything was passed down orally because we never learned to write."

I tilted my head and considered the woman. "You can't write? Can you read?"

Camilla lowered her gaze. "My mother taught me some words when she could sneak it past Master Carlton."

Dahlia squeezed Cami's shoulder. "We will have to change that. There are several apps that can help you learn."

Camilla's face went ashen and her movements were jerky as she grabbed some herbs from the cupboard. Dreya stopped her with a hand on her arm. There was the slightest pull back on Cami's part.

Having suffered at the hands of the former owner, Camilla used to flinch when others reached for her. I doubted she had ever experienced a kind touch before coming back as a ghoul.

"Do you want to learn how to read and write?" Dre was in tune in a way that the rest of us weren't, likely because as the eldest she had taken a mothering role with most of us.

I hadn't given it a second thought. Like my sisters, I assumed Cami would want to learn. Camilla turned and there were tears brimming in her eyes. The sight made my heart ache for her.

Cami nodded rapidly. "I would love that. I've already learned so much since coming back to life. I could actually become someone important. I never dreamed I'd have a life beyond being a slave to Master William."

"You already have a life beyond the Carltons. You are important to us and the business we are growing. In fact, you are vital to the success of the tours. The way you tell the stories is enthralling." I meant every word of what I'd said.

"Dani's right, Cami. You're one of us. An honorary seventh sister," Lia told the former ghoul. Honestly, I didn't know enough to know what she should be called now. Was she a normal witch again? "Before we get started on that, we need to find a woman before she gets killed."

Dreya and Dakota gaped at Lia. Kota crossed her arms over her chest. "What the hell are you talking about now? How are we supposed to find a murder victim and why do you even know about it? Is it more of your smell-o-vision at work?"

Lia sighed and ran a hand through her chin-length hair. "I had a vision of a dead woman being dumped on Canal Street after Dani and I met with Nedasea." Dahlia gave them a rundown of what she'd seen.

Dakota took the spoon from Lia and took a taste of the etouffee. "Alright, sestra. We've got your back. How can we help?"

It took me several seconds to comprehend what Kota had just said. She was typically wary and the last to offer to help. It irritated me at first, but I realized long ago that she had limitations to what she would do and it was okay. We each had strengths we brought to the group, and we needed to take advantage of them. Not force the others to do something they didn't want to do.

Dahlia sighed and sagged. "I knew I could count on you guys. I can't explain it, but this is something I have to do. From the moment Dani showed me this property, something clicked into place. This is where we are meant to be. And now, I know I am meant to use my new power to help others."

"So, in addition to owning a party planning business and tour company, we are supposed to be amateur detectives now?" I worked hard to hide my disbelief and wasn't sure I succeeded, given the way Lia narrowed her eyes.

Dahlia made a sound low in her throat. "I'm not saying that, Dani. What I am saying is there is a reason I was given the vision of this woman being dumped on the street. It wasn't to torment me. I have to save her. And yes, if that means we become private investigators, then that's what we do. You said it yourself. It's not like we can go to the police and tell them a woman will be killed in the future."

Dre cocked her head to the side. "I agree with you, Dahlia. You wouldn't be getting these visions unless the fates wanted you to do something about them. However, what about the supernatural police? There have to be officers that keep the magical world in line, right?"

Dre was level-headed and her points were valid, as were Dahlia's. I cringed, thinking of how insensitive I'd been. I understood how difficult it was to live with traumatic visions. Only mine were in the past and I *was* helpless to do anything about them. If I could have saved Camilla from even one second of pain, I would have.

A thought occurred to me as I silently berated myself for my less than supportive thoughts. "That makes sense. These powers have nothing to do with Phoebe and whatever she did to wake our genes up. Stella had none of this, and Phoebe gave her the power that made her a witch."

Dakota's forehead furrowed, and she chewed on her lower lip for a second. "Whoever is looking out for us went to a lot of lengths to get us in the position where we would buy Willowberry and be put in Phoebe's path, then have our powers unlocked. That doesn't seem accidental at all."

I inhaled a deep breath of garlic and spices. It made my stomach rumble. I crossed to the stove and looked in the pot. "That is entirely possible. I never believed the Greek gods existed until meeting Aidoneus. Do you suppose we could call Phoebe and have her ask him if the fates exist and, if so, could he ask them their plans for us?"

Lia laughed and shook her head. "There is no way we are calling to ask her boyfriend to talk to the fates. Based on everything I learned in college, they won't tell him anyway. They visit a person within three days of their birth and decide their destiny. They don't consult other gods and they don't explain themselves. Can you imagine that pressure?"

Dakota puffed out a breath. "Hell no, I can't. I don't want to decide anything for anyone else's life. Unless it's my kids. I don't mind whipping them into shape and getting them to pull their heads out of their asses."

"How many witches do you think are like us? Maybe there are others that can give us advice on how to handle the pressure. Especially if we are expected to become heroes. I don't think I can handle that kind of pressure." Dakota shuddered as she spoke.

"We should call Kaitlyn. She's our head witch. Certainly, she'll know and can give us some advice," I suggested. The woman had been nothing like I'd expected when we met her.

There was no pointy hat or striped, knee-high socks. And no wart on the end of her nose, which was a good thing because growths were not a good look. I was made for wide-brimmed beach hats and sandals.

Dahlia nodded in agreement and grabbed her phone off the charger on the built-in desk on the side of the kitchen. Camilla turned down the stove and joined us at the table as we sat down.

From the time we met her, she was attached to us. It was like a baby duck imprinting on a pack of wolves because they were there when she was born. Most days I worried we would be the death of Cami. Our lives had become unpredictable and dangerous since our awakening. I loved every second of it.

The jury was still out on how my sisters felt. The surface rarely showed what was happening in their hearts and grey matter. I knew Lia was happy with our lives. Surprisingly, Dakota, as well.

And Dreya and Steve seemed happy to be on the plantation. Steve had set up his distillery and was busy making *Mister Steve's Bayou Bourbon*. Deandra and Delphine weren't as big of a part of things yet because they still held full-time jobs and had young kids at home that needed them.

"Hey, Twisted Sisters!" Kaitlyn's voice snapped me back to attention and made my heart skip a beat. "How can I help you today?"

Dahlia chuckled, along with Dre and Kota. "Hi, Kaitlyn.

It's Lia and I'm here with Dreya, Dakota, and Dani. Camilla is with us, too. We have a few questions if you have time."

"I've got time, just give me a second to finish one thing and I will be all yours." The sound of fabric rustling against the speakerphone before the sound cut out.

"What do you think she does all day? Maybe she's like the police of the witches," Dreya suggested.

I snorted. "That sounds worse than being on the transport team for the NICU. At least there I encountered a set of expected crises. Yes, there was a crap ton of unpredictability and I was always on my toes, making split-second decisions to save a life, but none of it was magical. Based on what we've encountered so far, this world is one surprise after another."

Dreya nodded in agreement. "It was the same in the nursing home. I like the way this magic thing keeps us on our toes. It's one adrenaline rush after another. I've missed that since I left nursing a decade ago."

"The high goes away as soon as you adjust to your magic," Kaitlyn interjected, startling us all. Cami jumped the highest, and squeaked like a mouse about to be eaten by a fat cat.

"What about all the crap that keeps happening to us?" Dakota asked. "Will it stop? And, is there a supernatural police force? We have an emergency situation and don't know who to go to for help."

"There is a paranormal police force, but there aren't many agents. They tend to travel where they are needed for cases, but don't linger long. Although, there are some hotspots where agents have been assigned permanently. What's the problem?"

Lia sucked in a deep breath and told the head witch about what happened earlier. "I need to do something to find her and make sure this doesn't happen. That is only part of the reason we called you, though. How many witches are there with powers like ours? We're in over our heads and need help managing them and thought that others with more experience would be the best resource for that."

"There aren't many witches with powers like yours. In fact, I've only known one in my lifetime with premonitions and another that had psychometry. What powers do the others have?"

Dre leaned toward the phone Lia had set in the middle of the table. "I can move objects with my mind and Phi can freeze them. You already know Kota can materialize anything she wants, and Dea sees ghosts."

"All of those are rare powers, less than one in a thousand at the highest. However, seeing spirits is nothing special. All magical beings can see them. Has Phoebe been able to determine what you guys are?"

I scowled at the phone as if the head witch could see me. "Phoebe had no idea, and Aidoneus said we had Fae blood. Although I got the sense he thought there was more to us."

"Are you showing other powers? Have any of you set anything on fire?"

Dahlia's head jerked back and her eyes went wide. "What do you mean, have we set anything on fire? Of course not. Why would we do that?"

Kaitlyn laughed and her voice cracked as it came through the tiny speaker. "Young witches lose control of their witch fire when they go through puberty. It's a rough time for us and I figure you six are at a similar stage of development magic-wise."

"What is witch fire? Does that mean we can conjure flames?" The idea terrified yet exhilarated me at the same time.

"I love your enthusiasm," Kaitlyn observed. "You will be able to create flames, whether you are a witch or Fae. Fire is one of the four elements. But witch fire is different. That is unique to the individual. I would like to set up a time to get together with you and see what we can discover. I can run through spells with you and try to determine if you are a part witch."

A smile spread over my face as relief washed over me. "That would be amazing. Deandra and Delphine will be here the day after tomorrow. Otherwise, you can work with the four of us."

"I can make it then. If you have any other questions between now and then give me a call. Oh, and for the record, being the head witch is a full-time job. I do police witches. Most days it's like herding cats." Kaitlyn laughed before she said goodbye and hung up the phone.

I got up and grabbed a clean spoon and scooped up a bite of etouffee. My stomach was rumbling and it smelled delicious. I really hoped I liked it. Being picky was boring and got old. Not that my taste buds would get on board with me wanting change.

"We should call Phi and have her get the details down for Nedasea's party. We can't forget about our clients while looking for this mystery woman." My stomach wobbled as I brought the spoon to my mouth.

Garlic and onions exploded on my tongue. Then came the slightly fishy taste from the crawfish. Ugh. I spit it out and started coughing. Dahlia, Dakota, and Dreya were laughing.

Kota handed me a bottle of water. "I love that you always try new things, even if you don't like them. One of these days, we will find something new for you to add to your fried chicken and bean burritos."

"Damn straight we will." I really hope I came to love something new because I can't stand eating the same five or six things over and over. "Now, call Phi, would you Lia? We need to get the details down and come up with a work plan for this party, then we can shift gears back to your smell-o-vision."

Dahlia dialed the number, and Phi's chipper voice echoed through the kitchen. I had never been happier to have her there to document and keep us organized. My mind went in so many directions so fast that I needed her to keep track of the details. I could do it for myself, but it was chaos for my sisters as we prepared for and threw the parties.

The fates seemed to be thinking about their well-being when they gave my parents Delphine. Perhaps Dahlia was onto something there. The Six Twisted Sisters couldn't have been a more complete, cohesive group if I'd designed it myself. I hadn't considered that fact before that moment.

I sent a silent thank you to the infamous Moirai for giving me my sisters and a mother that taught us to work hard and persist until we reached our goal. Thanks to her, we understood the meaning of you can accomplish anything you set your mind to.

CHAPTER 4

Dahlia

The roller glided over the painter's tape Dani put on the wall to designate where to stop painting. "Crap."

A swipe of black went up in an arch. Now I needed to paint the orange stripe again. My mind was too busy replaying the scene I'd been sucked into when I was in the French Quarter the day before to pay attention to what I was doing.

I set the roller in the tray and grabbed a clean brush and the gallon of orange paint. Forcing my mind to the matter at hand, I tried to imagine the look Dani had for this room. No matter how hard I tried, I just couldn't put it all together.

The funky white wallpaper with orange and black accents looked great on the back of the built-in bookshelves. It was the thick stripes of matching color on the walls that I struggled with. I'd cut out one of her favorite sayings about being afraid to do something for fear of falling and doing it anyway because you might fly, to paint on the blocks of color.

Imagining individual pieces coming together was not my forte. I was a visual person and needed to see what it would look like when done. I was creative in many ways, but décor and design weren't on my list.

Wiping the sweat from my forehead with the back of my arm, I approached the black stain and attacked it with a vengeance. The hot flash that had hit me encompassed me in a bear hug, increasing my perspiration. They plotted their moment and launched a sneak attack at the worst possible moment. Thankfully, I wasn't yet under constant siege, like Dreya. I had a few more years before that happened.

The first coat of orange mocked my attempt to cover the dark stripe. Grabbing the heat gun from a hall closet, I plugged the thing in and really started sweating. I had to pause in my efforts and open the window to let in some cool spring air. Thankfully, it didn't get hot in New Orleans until May.

Weapon in hand, I attacked the black again. The second coat was better. The black, however, refused to give up. Like a two-year-old intent on getting ice cream for dinner, it decided to give one last hurrah.

With the heat gun back in hand, I dried that layer, pleased I'd almost beaten it into submission. I was applying one last coat when Lucas entered the room. His sexy scent preceded him, making my heart skip a beat.

The shifter was like the north pole and I was a magnet drawn to him. But I had no desire to see him fight with his ex. It was bad enough that I'd discovered that she'd left him and their daughter when she got caught up with drugs. It would be better if I didn't get involved with Lucas but the heart wants what the heart wants. I just couldn't seem to stop myself from spending time with him or wanting to be with him.

I released the breath I'd been holding when I wasn't overcome with dizziness. "Hey there. What can I do for you, good sir?"

Lucas growled low in his throat. "You can come out and have a picnic with me."

I'm not certain what I'd expected him to say. He'd expressed an interest in me before but had never asked me out, so I assumed he'd gotten a glimpse of the road map on my stomach. It would lead him to many places. The trouble was the road to heaven was obscured by the rest of them.

"I'm sorry. Did you just ask me to go have a picnic with you?" My hearing was fine most days, but like my cell phone after two years, it would stop working every once in a while. I was certain I had heard him wrong.

Lucas grabbed the paintbrush from me and set it on the tarp. "I made your favorite. Red beans and rice. I got the recipe from Camilla."

That piqued my interest. "How did you know that is my favorite? Did we have a conversation that I forgot about?"

Lucas's lips twitched. Was he rethinking his invitation? "I asked around. You have five sisters that were more than happy to share details with me."

I rolled my eyes. "Of course they were." They'd been on me to get back out there for years since Leo's death. It hadn't felt right. Until now. I picked up a rag and wiped the paint from my hands, then grimaced. I was covered in orange and black splatter.

"Let me wash up first. I'm filthy."

Lucas prowled toward me. My mind fritzed, and I forgot my name for a second. "I like you dirty. I find a woman that works with her hands sexy. Especially when she isn't afraid of getting dirty in the process."

I barely contained the shiver his words elicited. He made me want to grab the chop saw and start cutting the pieces for the crown molding. "Just wait until I get to the arbor in the garden. I'll be covered in filth when I scrape it clean and refinish it."

"Now you're just teasing me." He gestured to the door behind him. "Shall we?"

My feet were moving before my mouth. Although it wasn't far behind. It rarely is. "I could eat. However, I'm washing my hands first."

His chuckle followed me to one of the fifteen bathrooms a few feet away. My body tingled as his energy reached out to me. The cold water was a relief when it hit my hands. After scrubbing my digits clean, I splashed my face and scrubbed as if my life depended on it.

It wasn't until I lifted my head and saw a raccoon staring back at me I remembered I was wearing mascara. I didn't wear much makeup in general. A little on my eyes and some gloss. Having Lucas on the property, I'd started putting it on daily, so he didn't think I was totally hopeless.

My heart started racing as I realized I was in the one bathroom that was filled with decorative towels. Did I risk a lecture from Dani? Or use the bottom of my shirt? I was keenly aware of Lucas watching me from the doorway.

Deciding my sister owed me, I picked up a towel and wiped under my eyes until my face felt I'd taken an orbital sander to it. Lucas shook his head. "You look beautiful, as always."

At least he couldn't see the blush that stained my cheeks. "What made you want to have a picnic today?"

Lucas shrugged his shoulders. "I couldn't wait anymore to take you out. I wanted to show off my skills in the kitchen and impress you, so a picnic seemed like a good idea. Do you not like to eat outdoors?"

I sensed uncertainty in his question, which settled my nerves quite a bit. I wasn't a twenty-something, he knew that. Knowing he was in the same boat as me helped. "I enjoy it unless it's hot outside. Normally, I never have the chance. Before we bought Willowberry, I worked full-time with social services. I barely had time to eat in my car between home visits and court."

Lucas led the way down the hall behind the grand staircase and out the backdoor. I glared at Dani and Cami as we passed them in the kitchen. Noah was talking to Fred when we exited the house and headed to the parking lot.

Lucas grabbed a baseat, along with a blanket, then twined his free hand with mine. "Is the south part of the garden alright?"

I pursed my lips and pointed to the grass behind the massive garden close to the house. "How about we head out there? It's far enough away my nosy sisters can't spy on us."

Lucas chuckled. "Careful. You keep talking like that and I might get ideas."

I rolled my eyes while my heart raced and my palms started sweating. Great, now he was going to know I impersonated the swamp thing on the side. "Did my sisters tell you what happened after we met with Nedasea?" It was easier to ignore the innuendo. A date was one thing. I wasn't ready to go there, yet.

His head swiveled in my direction as we passed through the back of the garden. "They didn't say a thing. Did Brezok come on to you?"

My jaw went slack while I wondered why he would think such a thing. "Umm, no. Is that something I should worry about? We talked about working together when we have paranormal clients."

Lucas released a breath and shook his head. "He's been known as a lothario."

I could not imagine being attracted to the fame demon for a second. "Thankfully, he was on his best behavior. I had a vision while walking down Canal Street, and I'm hoping you can help with the case. We have no idea where to start investigating."

Lucas stopped us and spread the blanket on the ground. "What did you see?"

I sat on the edge of the blanket and crossed my legs like a pretzel. "It was nighttime and a guy with broad shoulders dumped a dead woman in front of one of the hotels. It had to be after two in the morning, given the lack of tourists. Her chest had been clawed open. It was awful."

Lucas looked up from taking the food from the basket. "What can you tell me about this guy? Aside from being big, what did he look like?"

I wrapped my arms around myself. "I didn't get a good look at him. He had on black clothes. And his car needed a new muffler, I think, because it was loud. I don't know how to control the visions or get better glimpses of the individuals involved, yet. I have to do something to save her and I'm hoping since you're in charge of all the shifters, I thought maybe you could help me find the guy. Or the girl."

Lucas sat down next to me and pulled me to his side. "I'm not in charge of all the shifters, Flower, just the ones here in New Orleans. A lot of them wear black and look like linebackers, so that isn't helpful."

"Are they all wolves?"

He kissed the top of my head, then continued pulling food from the basket. "No, there are jaguars, bears, and some other cat shifters. However, over seventy percent are wolves. No one under my purview would kill someone like that. They'd know I would find them and skin them alive."

I cringed and moved away from him. The imagery was violent and unpleasant. He put a hand on my leg. "I forget you aren't used to our world. Punishment in our world is swift and severe for something of this nature. If we don't, we run the risk of having more go rogue. Maintaining control over my shifters is my number one job."

That made sense and I felt bad for moving away from

him. "That's why there aren't very many paranormal police. You guys' police your own."

Lucas inclined his head and opened a plastic container. Rich spices drifted from the red beans, making my mouth water. "That's correct. Were you hoping to get police help with this vision? The rice is on the bottom."

I took the container from him and accepted a spoon. "Going to the police with a crime like this is all I know to do. Unfortunately, I can't go to the regular cops. All I have to go on is a loud car, a big guy, and a dead woman with sandy brown hair. That isn't much."

"I will help you however I can, but for now, can you set it aside and enjoy a meal with me?"

I stirred the beans and sausage, mixing the rice with it. "I can do that. What do you think of these buildings back here? We were hoping to overhaul them and rent them out."

Lucas ate his food and shifted his gaze to the low, long buildings about twenty feet away. "They haven't ever been updated, so it could take significant work. I imagine it will improve the energy of the plantation significantly to give these a new life."

A moan slipped from me as I chewed a savory bite and enjoyed the spice of the andouille. "Why would that improve the energy of Willowberry?"

"Slaves lived in those buildings. As you know, they weren't treated well by their owners. Those who lived there took pride in their homes and did what they could to keep them in good condition. I like to believe when we show the property the same love and attention the spirits can feel it."

My heart melted hearing his sensitivity. Few men were that in tune with how others felt, let alone ones that died centuries before. "I hadn't thought of it like that, but I like the sentiment. I'd do anything to improve their afterlife even a little. When I hear stories from Cami, it makes me sick to my stomach."

The weathered walls looked more like a slotted spoon than a house. I could see the other ones through the first one. The roof of the one closest to us had collapsed in one section. The windows were all missing, and the porch had given up long ago and was lying on the ground.

"Before you mentioned making the ghosts happy, I would have said the project is too much and given up. I'm not so heartless to quit now. Is it possible to shore up the bones with new supports? I wonder if we can refinish the original floors." My mind went through how long it would take to get these done.

Lucas waved his spoon through the air as he gestured to the homes. "Most will likely have dirt floors. Those that happened to have wood floors installed at some point will be saved. There will no doubt be holes to patch with pieces of antique reclaimed wood flooring. One thing is certain, I wouldn't dream of ripping the floors out entirely. Not when I see your eyes light up like that. I've never seen a more gorgeous sight."

A goofy grin spread across my face at the same time it heated from his praise. "The red raccoon look I'm rocking is going to be a new trend in Hollywood. Just wait and see."

Lucas chuckled and pressed a gentle kiss to my lips. "Your beauty is too good for those self-absorbed assholes. Not enough silicone or botulinum toxin."

"I should submit it to the top makeup artists. Maybe then we can afford to do the work out here. We're strapped as it is and can't take on another project. But it's good to know it is possible." My excitement over refurbishing the floors was short-lived as reality struck with a massive blow.

There was an ache in my chest as I refocused on the food.

"You did an amazing job on this. It's even better than Camilla's."

Lucas set his food aside and cupped one of my cheeks. It was hard to swallow the food in my mouth as my body leaned toward his. I felt like a teenager with a crush. I couldn't resist him.

"I will rebuild these houses with you, no matter how much it costs or how long it takes. We will start as soon as you're done in the main house, as well as Dreya's."

"Your willingness to help means the world to me. However, we don't have the money to purchase the supplies we will need. It's going to have to wait until we have more room in the budget. The money Phoebe paid us went to the roof on the main house and it helped us get the main kitchen finished quicker than we could have ever hoped for, which were our biggest expenses, but there are still a hundred smaller projects, as you know."

"This is going to happen, Flower. I will make sure of it. I will tarp the roofs as soon as we finish the barns closer to your house, then we can tear out walls so I can reinforce the supports. The good news is the foundations shouldn't be a problem since most were built right on the ground. The rest can be done as we have time and money."

My heart skipped several beats with his promise. It was clear by his tone of voice that he meant business. "Why would you go to this expense and trouble for me? If it's to get on my good side, you don't need to. I like you."

Lucas turned so he was sitting facing me fully. "I can see how much this means to you. Besides, it's been a long time since I was able to be part of something this important. And the best part is getting to do this with you. Putting that gazebo up with you made me want to do more projects together. Why else do you think I've been taking so long to get the work done?"

So many emotions ran through me with joy and amusement at the front. "I figured Noah couldn't bear to be away from Dani for very long. He seems to have fallen for her pretty hard. I also assumed you saw how much potential work there was in a plantation this run down."

Lucas laughed at that. "Noah is in deep with your sister. Thankfully, I found someone in the same location, or he would be a miserable guy to work with daily. You and your sisters brought this place back to life. It's vibrant and alive now."

I got lost in Lucas's grey eyes. My body had a mind of its own and leaned toward him at the same time he closed the distance between us. He stopped so close to me I felt his breath on my lips. My lips parted and my eyes started to slip closed in anticipation of his kiss.

Lucas pulled away, making me frown. What just happened? He inclined his head to the left. "We have visitors."

I followed his gaze. I rubbed my eyes, certain I was seeing things. "What in the world?"

There were five tiny faeries. That was the first thing that popped into my head. They were less than a foot tall and had iridescent wings beating as fast as a hummingbird's wings.

"They're pixies. I wonder what they're doing here. They rarely leave their lands."

My heart was pounding for a different reason now. I was torn between disappointment that the kiss was interrupted and fascination over our visitors. "Do they live here on Willowberry?"

Lucas shook his head from side to side. "No. I would have smelled their mound if they had one on your property. Plus, the previous curse would have been a deterrent to them. Having pixies show up now is considered a good sign."

"Like when a dragonfly lands on you?"

Lucas smirked. "I suppose so."

I watched the tiny beings hover several feet away and watch us. The best part of our new life was discovering mythical creatures were real. I never could have dreamed up such elaborate creatures. I couldn't get a good look at their wings because they were moving too fast, but if their pointed ears and jewel-colored hair were anything to go by, they were gorgeous.

CHAPTER 5

Danielle
"Why would she text nine-one-one when she's out here on a picnic with Lucas? It's not very romantic to call your sisters in for reinforcements." I knew Lia struggled to move on after Leo died, however, I thought she was past the guilt and ready to live again.

Dreya's face furrowed as we walked to the back forty of our property, where I wanted to tear down the buildings and reclaim the wood to make laser engraved signs to sell in the gift shop. Lia wanted to overhaul them and rent them out. Dreya agreed with her. Thankfully, we didn't have money to redo it at the moment, so we wouldn't continue to have the debate.

I had a difficult time adjusting what I envisioned, to include what others wanted. That presented a problem at times with clients, which is where my Twisted Sisters came into play. They knew it took me time to let go of what I wanted and reroute the info in my brain. I always gave the clients what they wanted, even if I didn't think it would be as cute as what I suggested. The situation with these buildings was no different.

"Do you think there could be another necromancer on the property? Kaitlyn promised we were warded against those that meant us harm. But without seeing proof, I had my doubts."

I shot Dre a look, and we both kicked our asses into gear. If she was in trouble and got hurt because we were taking our sweet time, I would never forgive myself. I wasn't in the best of shape. Too much time spent in a hospital and not enough on the treadmill, but I managed to keep up with Dreya, who ran marathons regularly.

We slowed when we saw Dahlia sitting on a blanket with Lucas. The scene would have been cozy if you ignored the tiny people hovering ten feet in the air in front of them.

"What the hell?" Dreya's words were muttered under her breath, but the paranormals in the group heard her because not only did Lucas's head turn our way, but the tiny faeries as well. "We better tell Dakota or she will be pissed she missed this."

Kota definitely preferred to be part of things, and this was something huge. It wasn't every day you met faeries. I whipped out my phone and shot off a text for her to get here right away.

Dahlia looked over as I was finishing, obviously reacting to the supernaturals. She lifted a hand. "We have company, and I didn't want to talk to them without you guys. It's incredibly good luck to have pixies pay us a visit."

I was glad Lia saw fit to inform us what the creatures were called. The last thing I wanted to do was offend para-normals who might become allies and/or clients. I inclined my head and paused by the blanket. It turned out the pixies weren't hovering ten feet in the air after all. They were just above the eye line for Lucas, who was sitting down.

Feeling like a giant next to the tiny beings, I knelt on the edge of the blanket. "Hi, I'm Dani, Dahlia's sister. And this is our other sister, Dreya. It's good to meet you." I lifted one finger and waved.

Dreya joined me and lifted a hand. "We have three other sisters that you might meet eventually. What brings you to Willowberry?"

A young woman with lime green clothes and blue hair flew closer to us. "I am Talewen. This is Ceisella, Jeiln, Adern, and Janoac. I assume she is Dahlia. Is the shifter your mate?"

Lucas's body shifted closer to Lia. "Dahlia and I are together. She and her sisters are new to the magical world and they need to feel their way through these situations and are unaware of the proper way to do things. It's best to be frank with them."

Lia coughed and sat up straighter. "Lucas is right. I suppose staring at you the way I did was incredibly rude. I meant no offense. You are just the most beautiful creatures I have ever seen.."

I was still putting names to the faces as my sister spoke with the pixies. If I wasn't mistaken, Jeiln had sapphire hair and was wearing beige clothes, while Ceisella had magenta hair and wore dark grey clothing. They were clearly female. If I had to guess, I'd say the other two were male. Adern had bright green hair that was a sharp contrast to his brown clothes. Janoac's blue clothing highlighted the rest of his features. His skin, hair, and eyes were all stunning shades of brown.

Dreya shifted and sat cross-legged. "What brings you to Willowberry? Are you here to ask us to host a party for you?"

Ceisella buzzed forward with a smile on her face. "There has been talk about your parties, but we are not here for the purpose. We are here to ask about forming an alliance."

Lucas held out his hand and gestured to the food set near

an open basket. "Please, join us. There is plenty of food. We can discuss the particulars while we eat."

I cocked my head and considered how he worded things. "Is there a formal way to conduct negotiations?"

I didn't want to get us into a mess with creatures we don't understand. From previous interactions, we were beginning to realize that very little in this world was simple or straight-forward. It's entirely possible I could end up bargaining away our land unknowingly.

Lucas pulled out a bowl of fruit and took off the lid, setting it out for the pixies. They flew to the blanket and perched on the handle of the basket. "There is a formality to everything. However, the shifter has informed us to speak plainly. Normally, we would present an offering and provide proof of what we can offer you before making our request," Talewen explained. "Of course, if you prefer to set up a future meeting, we will be prepared."

Dreya threaded her fingers together. "What kind of offer-ing? We aren't formal people. When planning an event, yes. We keep to traditions and are professional. In our personal lives, we're much more down-to-earth and open."

Ceisella pointed to a section of grass near her and waved her finger in a circle. "We would bring the fruits of our labor. Sometimes it's flowers or produce." A bright pink tulip sprouted through the ground where she'd pointed. "And others are gems and metals."

Janoac stood up and removed a brooch from the ocean blue vest he was wearing. The thing was an odd symbol I didn't recognize. It made me think of those ancient Viking runes that had become popular with my son. "We would also offer our master craftsman to assist or teach their trade."

Dahlia moved closer to examine the silver object. Janoac handed the brooch to her. "What do we give you in exchange for such wonderful gifts?"

I nodded in agreement. "If you are looking for protection, I'm afraid you are asking the wrong witches, er, Fae." It was incredibly embarrassing to not know what we were or what we could do exactly.

Talewen cleared her throat. "We are here to ask permission to move onto Willowberry Plantation and build our mound. We outgrew our old one and the five of us left together."

Dahlia's forehead furrowed. "You're homeless? How are you surviving? Are there no social services for paranormals? It's not like pixies can go out and get a job to pay for a new place."

Lucas chuckled and pressed his lips to the top of Dahlia's head. It was an intimate gesture and made me think of Noah and how familiar he was with me as well. It should be awkward and too fast for this type of behavior, but it wasn't. Neither of them was pushing us for more than we were ready to give, making it easier to accept their affection.

"Their situation is different than you think, Flower. They don't survive like you and I do. They build their houses underground and survive on the land. Where have you been living since moving from your previous mound?" Lucas was good for Lia. The way she lit up when he looked at her was something I hadn't seen, not since before she lost Leo.

Talewen looked up from picking up a strawberry that was as big as her head. "We've been living in the unclaimed swamplands."

Dre grimaced and shook her head. "Why would you want to live in a place like that? Your powers seem anathema to such a location."

Dahlia nodded. "Not to mention the alligators that would be happy to have you for a snack. Or perhaps you can use magic to protect yourselves from them."

"We are Fae. We have power over the elements and can

manipulate them to suit our purposes, but those creatures are relentless in their pursuit," Ceisella informed us with a full-body shiver.

"Living in the swamp takes a special kind of person. The pack lands are bordered on one side by a swamp, which we take advantage of during hunts. Otherwise, we steer clear. And we ensure our kids do the same. We lost more than one pack member to the gators. Why would you settle out there? Its dangers are no secret. Not to mention the fact that I know you can't be flourishing because you can't build a proper mound out there, like your kind requires."

My hackles went up hearing Lucas ask them this point-blank. Were they trying to manipulate us into allowing them on our land so they could take advantage of us? They were cute little people with wings, but that didn't mean they wouldn't manipulate situations to their advantage.

Talewen sighed and set her berry down. "We had no other choice unless we moved away from New Orleans. You know how populated the area is, especially closer to the French Quarter. There isn't enough land to sustain us. We're symbiotic beings and need to share space with another magical being. The problem is in the Garden District where our old mound was located, there isn't enough space. We would have stripped the land trying to build anywhere close to there. Locations with ample space that are safe are dwindling."

"That's not surprising, given that it's located next to a concrete jungle," I observed. "Why not move out to Metairie? Or another city close by?"

"Many of our kind established mounds hidden on plantations back in the day and we have been searching for the right one for us," Talewen shared. "Again, few magical beings own property out here. They prefer to be closer to the action, so many of the previous mounds have been abandoned."

Dreya cocked one eyebrow. "Is there an empty one on Willowberry? Is that why you asked us?"

Ceisella shook her head, making her long magenta hair fly in every direction. "There has never been one on this land. It is sterile ground for our kind, as it has always carried a curse. The negative energy would have killed any who tried to build a home here. We're very sensitive to dark intentions."

These tiny beings looked like a stiff wind would crumple their wings. I imagined they couldn't tolerate much. It reminded me of working with premature infants in the NICU. Their systems were delicate and underdeveloped, which left them vulnerable to a multitude of things.

"And the energy is now suitable for your needs?" Dahlia asked as she watched Talewen pick up the berry and bite into it.

The blue-haired pixie wiped the juice off her chin with the back of her hand and moaned as she chewed. "It is recovering at a rapid pace. That is something we can help accelerate if you allow us to make a home here."

Ceisella took the fruit from Talewen and took a bite. I watched as the small winged woman ate some of the pink flesh as well. With wide eyes, she handed it to Adern. I got the impression it had been some time since they'd eaten anything this fresh.

Dahlia shot me a questioning look. I shrugged my shoulders. I had no idea if it was a good idea or not. They seemed genuine and had shown no sign of being a threat. She turned her attention to Dreya, who nodded her head.

"What's this about pixies? Where are they?" Dakota was running in our direction and was slightly out of breath. It was clear she dropped everything and hurried right over. Dreya gestured to our guests with her open hand.

Kota came to a stop and bent over, bracing herself with

her hands on her knees while she caught her breath. "Oh, my Gods. You weren't kidding."

Dreya introduced Dakota and gave her a rundown of their request. Dakota knelt down closer to the basket and held out a hand. "We would be honored if you made your home here. Would you be willing to help cultivate flowers for parties we throw? Not for everyone, but some of the bigger ones."

My mind was so busy trying to find the pixie's angle that I hadn't considered asking for this in return. It would be outstanding to be able to offer pixie-grown flowers to our clients. *Not that you can tell the humans about their magic.* That was a valid point. Our paranormal customers would love it.

Talewen shot into the air along with her fellow pixies. "We can do that. We will need enough notice so we don't leech the magic and nutrients from the soil. We can take over all the gardening on the property."

"Fred has worked on the plantation for decades. I would hate to let him go," Dreya interjected. I had to agree. He was a nice man and had done a great job keeping the property in shape by himself. "In terms of the parties, we usually have a few months to a year's notice."

Janoac pursed his lips. "We have seen him working tire-lessly on the grounds. What if we assisted him behind the scenes and made it easier for him to maintain? Doing so will help us create and deepen a connection to this land."

Lucas chuckled. "The guy could use the help and wouldn't be surprised if you worked beside him. He's sensitive to magic and in tune with more than most mundies. He knows Noah and I are different, but has never pushed the issue."

Lia sighed and put the plastic bowl on top of the basket where the pixies had once again perched. They'd been eyeing the food since Lucas pulled it out. "Fred warned us the plantation was cursed the very first day we moved in, so that isn't surprising. What else have you been watching?"

I gestured to the fruit. "I can see your hunger. Eat." I picked up a blueberry and handed it to Jeiln. Our fingers touched, and I sucked in a breath. Everyone around me disappeared. Instead, in front of me, I saw the group of pixies shivering as they huddled together in a tree.

There was water below them and several gators watching them from the murky depths. Talewen handed Jeiln a pepper of some kind, saying it was the last one she could find. The group each took a bite before tossing the stem.

I'd been sucked into the past enough times I was familiar with it. My sisters were, too. A hand landed on my shoulder as Dreya called my name. I blinked and shook my head. "I'm alright."

"What did you see?" Lia's gaze shifted from me to the pixies, knowing I'd seen something about them.

"You guys have been starving. Why didn't you approach sooner?" My heart ached for their plight. I was glad we'd already agreed to help them.

Lia gasped and picked up her container of red beans and rice, then shoved it at the pixies. "Lucas invited you to eat. If you are hungry, eat whatever you want. We have plenty more back at the main house, as well."

Talewen's cheeks turned pink, and she lowered her head. Lucas cleared his throat. "That is not a judgment on your ability to lead your clan. The sisters are the kindest women I have ever met. Their concern is as genuine as their offer of help. They understand what it is like to have nothing and struggle to survive."

Dahlia nodded in agreement. "I admire your courage in coming to us with your proposition. It couldn't have been easy to take a risk when you know nothing about us."

Janoac's cheeks blushed. "Dreya asked what else we'd

been watching before Dani had her vision. We have been watching you six interact with each other and those around you. We know Lucas tells the truth from our observations. The magic you have worked on the land is undeniable. You've even improved conditions in the river that leads to the swamp."

Talewen inclined her head. "That is why we have approached you. We were about to move out of the area when the Pleiades unlocked your magic. It intrigued us]she was able to accomplish such a feat with you."

I lifted one eyebrow as the pixies began nibbling on the food. "What do you mean that she was able to *accomplish such a feat* with us?"

"There has never been another case of a witch awakening dormant magic in a mundie. Your bloodlines are diluted enough that you previously exhibited no power. Phoebe shouldn't have been able to do what she did," Lucas interjected. "You six are uncharted territory. We have no idea what exactly you are or how powerful you will become."

Dahlia shook her head. "It wasn't just Phoebe. The bees swarmed around us. I had a hundred stings all over me."

Dakota lifted a finger into the air. "It could have been Phoebe. She made her best friend a witch when she was just a normal person."

Talewen approached Dahlia and held a hand out. Dahlia touched a finger to the middle of her small palm. "The Pleiades cannot make a Fae and you are at least part-Fae."

Dakota sighed and grabbed a roll from the food and broke off a piece. She was a bit of a nervous eater. "So, we know we're part-Fae. We'd guessed that much from what Aidoneus said. Can you tell if we are more?"

Talewen shook her head from side to side and returned to the basket. "That is beyond my abilities."

Dreya stood up and brushed off her jeans. "Where will

you build your mound? What do you need from us? How do we help you with your project?"

I almost groaned. We did not need to add more to our to-do list. Not that I was going to deny these tiny creatures help. I would do what we needed to do. Then I was going to take a nap. We'd moved from the air mattresses a week ago, but I wasn't sleeping well in a room by myself. I found it impossible knowing there was a ghost haunting the halls.

"We will handle the structure with our earth magic. We would like to establish the mound out here amongst these buildings and trees. They will provide us cover and give us fertile ground." Talewen's words were music to my ears.

We invited the pixies back to the main house for more food so they could meet Dea and Phi, who were on their way after their shifts ended. Our family was already big but it seemed, since moving here we just kept adding to it.

It was fitting, given that our mom always welcomed others to our house and our table when she already had twelve mouths to feed and care for. She never turned away a friend in need or denied them a hot meal. We wouldn't do so either.

CHAPTER 6

*D*anielle
Delphine set her fork down and wiped her mouth. "I cannot freaking believe there are pixies living at Willowberry. Rachel will freak out when she sees them. They're so tiny. Are we sure they're alright living outside? We have plenty of rooms inside the house."

I had wondered the exact same thing and even asked Talewen to make sure. I'd seen how cold and hungry they'd been in the bayou. "Now that they have a place here at the plantation, they are able to build a safe house and start over. They had it rough for a bit after they left their previous mound. Seeing them shaking harder than the leaves in the tree was awful."

Lia sipped her margarita before setting it down. "I keep thinking about how many strings the fates had to have put in place for everything to line up as they have. If we hadn't purchased this place, they might have died out there in the swamp, unable to find a safer location away from here."

Dakota rolled her eyes. "Don't be so dramatic, Lia. They're magical creatures. I don't know why they stayed in the swamp like that, but they did. Any suffering is on them. They can fly! They could have gone anywhere for dinner. There was no need to go hungry."

"Actually, I don't think that's true. There aren't many places they could go without being seen and recorded. The one thing that has been made clear to us since we got these powers is that we need to keep the magical world a secret," Dre pointed out.

Deandra nodded her head in agreement. "That's right. Everyone with a mobile phone is looking to go viral or thinks they're a YouTube star and records everything. Besides, they don't have money from what they told us. They couldn't just fly to the closest restaurant and grab some food."

Dakota tilted her head as she chewed another bite of her enchiladas. "Alright, I'll give you that. They also said they depend on another paranormal to survive, which is why they wanted to make their home here. I imagine in exchange for their services and gems, witches like us buy them food they can't grow. What about their clothes? Do you think they wear doll clothes? They weren't made from leaves or anything."

Dea's bark of laughter spurned the rest of us, as it typically did. Even Camilla had joined in the amusement. Deandra was the only person I knew that could do that, regardless of the situation. I doubled over and squeezed my legs together while the giggling fit continued.

Dea wiped her eyes as she subsided. "Barbie's clothes have become rather stylish. The shoes, though. Those things would never work for them."

"Those wouldn't work. Barbie's clothes have no shape, the girl pixies had more curves than I do. I bet they make their clothes. It's the only thing that makes sense," Phi observed.

I did a mental check of the state of my underwear,

relieved the laughter hadn't made me tinkle. Camilla got up and started gathering the plates. "Pixies are supposed to be the best seamstresses and metalsmiths on the planet. At least they were in my time."

Mary Alice floated through the ceiling, stopping next to her daughter, making us jump in our seats. "Camilla is correct. I used to buy most of my gowns from a woman that had a pixie working for her."

Cami shot her mother a scowl. Dahlia stood up to help with the dishes and we all joined in. Mary Alice seemed to get the picture when we all exited the dining room. Kota leaned closer to me. "Do you think she will follow us? She gives me the creeps."

I snorted. "Tell me about it. It keeps me up at night. But she won't follow. She knows Cami doesn't want her around. I have to give it to her, though. She keeps trying."

Delphine grabbed her tablet as soon as the dishes were in the dishwasher and we all retreated to the lady's parlor. It had become our favored place to hang out. I wasn't sure why we'd chosen that room out of all of them. It just felt natural to be in there. I assumed it had to do with the centuries of women that had gathered there.

"Shifting gears, let's talk Nedasea's party," Phi said as we sat down.

Dahlia's gasp was loud in the room. Was she having another vision? It seemed unlikely unless she had gained the ability to function during one because she was racing away from the window and out the door.

"What is it?" Dreya called after her.

"There's someone breaking into your house," Lia yelled out.

Delphine was out of the room next, with Dreya hot on her heels. Dakota and I were last and moving as fast as we could. Kota looked at me and I saw fear in her eyes. It was something I had only seen when our mom was diagnosed with cancer and told it was inflammatory breast cancer, stage four, and one of the deadliest kinds.

"Steve is in there alone. He can't battle a paranormal. He's just a normal guy." Dakota was right about that.

"Just because everything seems to revolve around magic now, doesn't mean it is paranormal," I reassured her.

My heart was racing and my chest constricted when I saw several individuals fighting outside Dreya and Steve's house. The noise of the bees was almost as loud as the grunts and shouting.

We hadn't made it very far when a low groan came from the right, making the hair on the back of my neck stand on end. The sound reminded me of the zombies in that popular TV show. It was exactly the same.

Dakota grabbed my hand and yanked on me. "What the hell is that?"

"I have no idea." I wanted to continue running to help Dreya and the others, but I couldn't ignore the way my gut was screaming at me that something was very wrong. "But it isn't good. Can you wish for a gun or something?"

Kota made a strangled noise. "Can you shoot a gun? I have no idea how to use a weapon like that."

I shook my head from side to side and wanted to curse. "A big ass knife then. You know, the ones they chop down bushes in the jungle with."

"I wish I had a machete." Dakota squeaked a second later and thrust the weapon at me.

I took the black handle and marveled for a split second at how it looked just like a really long knife from our cutting block. Holding it with two hands out in front of me, I scanned the dark yard. There were several willow trees lining what would be the main walk up to the front door, otherwise, the land was pretty clear until closer to the edge of our property. The first creature to come stumbling out from behind the trees along the walk made my stomach churn.

"Is that a damn zombie?" Dakota's voice trembled like my legs were at that moment.

"Yes. How are there freaking undead walking around the plantation? Doesn't the ward do anything?" I wanted to call Kaitlyn and curse at her for giving us a false sense of safety. The thing did nothing to help us.

"I wish I had a machete." I quirked an eyebrow at Dakota. She shrugged her shoulders. "I can't very well run back in the house when my sisters are out here facing danger. Go for the brains. They can't keep coming for us if they don't have heads."

I snorted and headed toward the things that looked worse than Camilla had when Phoebe first brought her back. "You watch too much television, sestra. I doubt it works like that in real life."

"It's worth a try. Haven't you heard that fiction resembles reality? How can anyone attack when they are missing their head? It's a good solution."

I cocked my head and watched as they lumbered slowly. This might be easy. "You're right. I've never decapitated anything before. I hope I don't throw up."

"You and me both," Kota agreed.

My knees automatically bent and I ran in a crouch toward the zombies while holding the machete in front of myself. I'd reached the first big tree and plastered my back against it.

The position gave me a view of Dakota hunched over and hurrying toward me. I must have looked like an idiot when I'd done the same thing. A yelp left me when sharp finger-nails scraped the skin of my shoulder. My heart started beating a million miles a minute as I brought the weapon up and slammed it down on the arm. The smell of meat left out in the sun for a week straight made bile rise to the back of my throat.

Despite the way vomit was playing tonsil hockey in my throat, I had the presence of mind to use my weapon. To my surprise, I met no resistance as the blade sliced through rotting bone. It sounded like a dry stick breaking.

I'd put so much force behind my swing that my arms shook when the tip hit the bark of the tree. The hand and part of the arm landed on the ground. I noted that there was no blood.

I stepped away from the trunk and yanked my machete free. Dakota came to stand by my side. "Did it break the skin? You'll become one of them if it did."

I rolled my eyes. I really hoped she was wrong about that because it had cut through my shirt and the top layers of flesh. Dancing forward, I swung out as I got close to the zombie that had injured me. The blade cut through the dried skin, tendons, and muscle tissue like they were paper.

My momentum carried me around in a circle and by the time I faced the zombie again, its head had rolled from his shoulders. Loud shrieks rent the air, piercing my eardrums. The sound was followed by an overwhelming stench of rotting meat. I thanked the gods I didn't have Dahlia's visions. No doubt this would have given her a doozy.

The undead creatures were no longer ambling awkwardly in our direction. It was as if they'd taken speed as they raced toward us. Dakota screamed, voicing how I felt. I braced my legs apart and swung at the first one to reach me.

Dakota was sobbing behind me. I took a step back as my blow knocked the zombie off its course. There were three more right behind him. My feet stopped as my arms became whirling dervishes. I hacked and hacked without stopping.

Soon I was overcome and knocked over. The machete

flew from my hand. There was a second when I was certain this was the end for me. I was going to die at the hands of these smelly undead creatures.

As if you would ever just lie here and give up. Use what your mama gave you. Right, I wasn't completely helpless. Lifting my legs wasn't easy. Have I mentioned how out of shape I am? The reverse crunch made my abs cry out in agony.

The sight of the zombies frantically trying to reach me made it easy to ignore my discomfort as I kicked out at everything I could. I managed to push most of them away from me within seconds and jumped back to my feet as if I was a ninja.

Once upright, I was glad to see Dakota still standing,swinging her machete. I punched a woman that was missing the lower half of her jawbone. The machete might cut through the bones with ease, but my fists couldn't do the same.

My knuckles were going to be bruised later, for sure. The woman grabbed hold of me right as I jumped to the side. Her fingers tangled through my hair and she pulled me off-balance. Landing on my ass, I had never been more grateful for those extra twenty pounds, as they cushioned the fall.

Silver glinted at the base of the closest tree. I scrambled forward and dove like I was stealing home base. The grass wasn't as soft as I expected, and I bounced a few feet rather than executing the smooth slide I had envisioned.

Regardless, I was within reach of the machete and snatched it up. I was not a badass warrior like Dahlia and Dreya could be. Flower arrangements and décor were more my speed.

Channeling my rage at having my property violated, I got up and swung. Dakota jumped out of the way when I over-reached, which allowed my blade to slice through the woman's skull where her mandible should have been.

I couldn't watch her head roll away. It wasn't that I was upset that I killed her. She was a zombie. She was already dead before I hit her, but my stomach could only handle so much. The maggots coming out of one of the zombie's eyes, coupled with the stench were making me sick. It was best not to push my luck.

I hacked at maggot-face but barely managed to remove a pinky finger before his fist collided with my left shoulder with a solid thud. The blow jolted me and made my eyes water.

"Dammit," I growled.

Rather than swing the weapon, I stabbed it at his head, aiming for the maggots. The blade slid right through the eye sockets and made a squishing sound. There was a sickening squelching as I pulled the machete free.

Dakota was right about going for their brains because this one crumpled in a heap. There were two more behind him, so I kept stabbing and swinging as they attacked. They weren't the brightest creatures.

Hot agony made me roar when something sliced my left collarbone. The area was already smarting from the previous hit it had taken. Now, though, it was on fire. With a growl, I lowered my blade and chopped the head in front of me down the middle, then turned to the one behind me.

This zombie looked fresher. Didn't smell like it, but she still had skin that wasn't completely rotten, so that was an improvement. I could see Dakota chopping at zombies around her with surprising ferocity. Of course, she swore like a sailor while doing it.

The wetness on the back of my shoulder was no doubt blood from the injury the freshie in front of me inflicted. I jabbed my weapon and danced forward, making her retreat. When her back was against the tree, I hefted the machete and brought it down at an angle.

The steel cut through her right shoulder blade and scapula, then several ribs and vertebrae. Surprisingly, my silver was no longer shiny, but stained with dark brown blood.

The zombie's eyes flared before the upper right section of her chest and her head fell to the ground. That was the straw that broke my nausea's back. The dinner we'd just eaten came rushing up through my esophagus and out of my mouth and nose.

I couldn't fight while I was hurling and the last zombie close to me took advantage by jumping on my back. Its claw-like nails dug into my wound and her mouth went for my neck. For the second time that night, my life flashed before my eyes.

Dakota's scream echoed right before she cut through my attacker's neck. The fear had driven back the remainder of the nausea, which allowed me to stand up and take stock. We were alive and whole, for the most part.

"Are you alright? We need to call Kaitlyn and find out if zombies are contagious. You were scratched several times." Dakota's agitation was obvious.

I scanned her, knowing adrenalin could mask severe injuries. There wasn't a drop of blood on her. "Are you alright? Did you get hurt?"

Kota sighed and kicked the torso of a zombie out of our way. "I'm alright. Let's check on the others and call Kaitlyn."

She wrapped her arm around my waist and supported me as we walked. I could have managed on my own. However, I didn't pull away, having sensed that she needed the contact.

"I've never killed anyone before." Her voice was small and it cracked as she spoke.

I hugged her close. "Me neither. We didn't really kill them, you know. They were already dead. Someone or something brought them back."

Talewen and Jeiln flew in our direction as we got closer to Dreya's house. "Thank the gods you two are alive. We thought you were in the house." Talewen stopped abruptly when she caught sight of my shoulder. "Jeiln, get the tincture. This wound needs to be treated before it gets infected."

The pixie with sapphire hair and grey eyes took off in the direction from which they came and swooped down to a leather bag next to Adern. Two feet from them were my other sisters and Steve, all sitting on the ground away from at least a dozen bodies. My heart slowed knowing they had survived the attack.

I turned my attention back to Talewen as she flew next to me. "Is there anything I need to worry about with this injury? I won't become like them, will I?"

The pixie shook her head from side to side. "You're not a mundie, so you will be fine once I neutralize the bacteria. If I don't, it will eat away at your skin until it eventually kills you."

I sucked in a breath. "You mean this is necrotizing fasciitis?"

"Zombies carry a fast-acting version of the deadly bacteria," Talewen clarified.

Dakota scrunched up her nose. "Who the hell sent these things after us, and how did they get past our wards?"

We reached Jeiln before she got back to us. I collapsed beside Dahlia, who had a few minor cuts and scrapes. Janoac was rubbing something on her cheek. It smelled like cilantro and a few other herbs. The tiny male pixie looked up and met my gaze. "Zombies are created by Voodoo magic. Your wards are strong, but Marie Laveau and her mambos have a way of getting past them with the right offering to one of their Loa."

Lia cursed and rubbed her temples. "Not only do we have a murder to prevent, we have to watch out for the most powerful woman in New Orleans? Just what we need right now."

Jeiln came toward me carrying a pouch and hovered behind me. The gel was cool and soothing when she applied it. "You need to work with the head witch. Your wards can be adjusted to prevent this from happening again. Marie isn't one to come at you outright. We know Phoebe upset her attempt to insert one of her gods into a ghoul. This might have been her tantrum over the incident. You can make it harder for her to get her creatures across the barrier and focus on the most urgent issue."

I twisted my neck around and gaped at the tiny pixie that had been the quietest of the bunch. "Thank you. Kaitlyn is already scheduled to come to test our magic with us. We can add this issue to the list."

Phi held up a finger. "I need to backtrack a bit. What's this about stopping a murder?"

Dahlia gave them a rundown of what she'd seen on Canal and how she felt it was her duty to save the victim. Deandra and Delphine's eyes got wider and wider. Finally, Dea stood up and crossed to one of the bodies. "We have dead zombies littering our land. Probably poisoning it, too. And you're telling me we need to find a needle in a haystack and locate an unknown woman and her equally anonymous killer?"

Phi stood up with Deandra and wrapped her arm around her waist. "We miss a lot while we're at work. We will handle this like we do everything else, together."

Dea nodded. "What do we do with these bodies?"

Lia grinned like the wicked witch. "We should pile them up on Ms. Laveau's doorstep when we go stake out the spot on Canal where the woman is going to be dumped."

Dreya sighed and laid her head on Steve's shoulder. "Why would we do either of those things?"

Lia shrugged her shoulders. "Because I don't want these

things tainting our land any longer, and we might run into the killer while we are hanging around."

Janoac's shout stopped all conversation. Phi threw her hands up and the pouch that had fallen from the pixie's grasp froze in mid-air. Dea gasped a second later and narrowed her eyes at Phi. "What did you do?"

"I don't know. I reacted to Janoac losing hold of his potion and it froze." Delphine moved closer to the bag and grabbed it out of the air.

Dea pursed her lips. "That wasn't the only thing you froze. There are three ghosts that have been paused, as well."

"Looks like the magic didn't skip you after all, little sis." Dreya's words made Phi flinch.

Delphine shook her head from side to side. "But I thought I was the normal one of the bunch. How is this possible?"

Dahlia reassured her while I let my eyes slip closed. I was exhausted and ready for bed. The pain of the injury had subsided. Whatever that tincture was, it worked wonders on my injury. I could have used that at the hospital.

"We will need to burn the bodies off your land within the hour or they will taint the ecosystem," Talewen announced.

So much for getting some rest. I sent another thank you to The Moirai for bringing the pixies into our lives. Without them, we would be calling Noah and Lucas or Kaitlyn. It was nice to be somewhat self-sufficient. I didn't like the idea of being so dependent on Noah when really I needed to learn to stand on my own two feet.

CHAPTER 7

Dahlia

My heart raced in my chest, and sweat damp-
ened my palms. I was still wide awake after the confronta-
tion with the zombies. To say we had been shocked by the
turn of events was an understatement.

We'd known taking a stance with Phoebe would be risky,
but we had done what we thought was right. There was no
way we could allow Laveau to hijack our ritual and take
away either ghoul's chance at life.

My training and experience told me Selene's story was
fraught with heartache and torment. Camilla had shared
more than one of her horror stories. The fact that her
mother was still hanging around spoke volumes about what
Cami went through. Both women deserved safety and security. No way would my sisters or I allow a sketchy Voodoo
Queen to take that away.

And, can I say what a disappointment it was to discover
Marie Laveau wasn't the woman of lore? She was far, far
worse. Growing up in New Orleans, you inevitably heard
stories about how Laveau used to help others with her

advice, herbs, and magic. The reality couldn't be more different.

Yes, Phoebe had explained this was a descendent of the original woman, which made it even worse in my mind. She should be upholding her ancestor's reputation, not tearing it down.

Stop stalling and call Lucas. With trembling fingers, I pulled up his contact on my cell and hit the button. The ringing seemed to echo through my body. Would he help me?

"I'm glad you called, Flower. I was just thinking about you." His voice soothed and excited me at the same time.

"You were?" For some reason, that surprised me.

He chuckled, sending shivers through me. "You are always on my mind. While I hope I'm on yours, I suspect that isn't the reason for your call."

I sucked in a breath. "Can you read my mind?" It was unnerving how the man knew what I was thinking most of the time.

"We're connected in ways you can't understand. What's wrong? What happened?"

His words made me want to ask what he meant, but I filed that away for another time. I needed to get this out before I chickened out. "I was hoping you would be willing to take me to the Quarter."

There was the sound of a door in the background. "Why? What do you want to do down there?"

"I was hoping to discover more about the dead woman. Or her killer. After Marie's zombies attacked, I couldn't sleep and figured now was as good a time as any."

"What? Marie attacked you guys? Is everyone alright?" His truck rumbled to life and competed with the growl in his voice.

I quickly told him what happened earlier. "Thanks to

Talewen and the others, our injuries are healing, and we'll have no complications from them."

"How do you know it was Marie?"

I scoffed. "Are you kidding? She's the queen of the dead, right? Who else would send them after us?"

A horn honked on his end, making me wonder how fast he was driving toward me. "In the magical world, you need to be very careful who you make accusations against and who hears it. The people you are dealing with are extremely powerful and will not take kindly to having their reputations marred. Marie is no exception. Any of her mambos would be capable of sending zombies after you guys."

Thank God we hadn't followed through with piling the zombies on her doorstep. Honestly, if we knew where she lived, we might have given it greater consideration. "This world is so foreign to all of us. Good thing we aren't planning on addressing that particular issue right now. I'm inclined to ignore it forever."

That seemed like the best option after what Lucas said about it upseting her if we confronted her, or if she caught wind that we had been accusing her. I was leaning toward the latter. The last thing we needed was her ire. Her power was terrifying. The only reason she hadn't done anything during the ceremony was that Phoebe had been there and she was more than a match for Laveau.

"You cannot ignore it. The magical world respects strength. You will need to take a stance, but it can wait. Please tell me the bodies aren't on your land. You will breed bacteria and dark energy. The curse will look like child's play if you bury a bunch of zombies on the plantation."

It was nice to know the pixies told the truth about what would happen if we left the bodies on the property. "The pixies informed us of what would happen and we drove them into the bayou and had a bonfire. They said that was preferable to burying them and leaving them to contaminate the area."

"You and your sisters have managed to draw powerful and valuable allies to your side. Your entire situation fascinates me. I have never seen anything like this in my life. You were mundies a couple of months ago with no knowledge of the magical world. Now you are powerful magical beings and have the Pleiades as a close friend. Not to mention a high witch and pixies establishing a new mound on your plantation. *And* you create the perfect parties."

I flushed hearing his praise and ask, "Is that why you like me? Because I'm an anomaly?"

It was Lucas's turn to snort. "That's not even a small part of why I like you, Flower. You're beautiful, courageous, talented, intelligent, sexy."

I laughed, cutting him off. "Okay, I get it. No need to go on." He'd proven his point and the more he said, the more uncomfortable I got.

I liked all the same things about him. Admittedly, I focused more often on how gorgeous he was. In my defense, he was built like an Adonis and perfect in every way. How could a girl resist getting lost in that body?

"Did I lose you, Flower?"

I wanted to say never but held my tongue. That was the danger in thinking about his sexiness. "No. I'm here."

"Alright. Did you want me to come up and get you, then?"

I jumped off my bed and stuffed my feet in my leather boots. "Sorry. I didn't hear you say you were here. I'm on my way out now."

Lucas's chuckle echoed through the phone as I hung up and hurried down the stairs. I had to make myself slow down when I hit the second floor. Arriving covered in a sheen of sweat would not be attractive.

To my relief, I didn't encounter Dani, Camilla, or her

mother as I left the house. Locking the back door, I noticed a greenish glow in the distance of our property. It was where the older, more rundown slave quarters were located. I hoped zombies weren't back and attacking the pixies this time.

A hand on my shoulder made me gasp. My hand flew to my chest where my heart was pounding a million miles a minute. "Sorry," Lucas whispered, his mouth close to my ear.

I sucked in a calming breath. "It's ok. I'm on edge after the earlier. Do you see that?" I pointed to the light.

Lucas nodded as he put his hand on my lower back and nudged me toward the parking lot. "That's the pixies working on their mound. Their magic glows when they expend a lot of it. And making a new mound will take everything they have collectively."

That was a freaking relief. I had no desire to battle those things again. It had been tough enough the first time. Dani and Dakota fared better because Kota conjured each of them with machetes. We'd had her conjure one for each of us. We stored them in Dreya's house, figuring it was the safest place given we would have visitors coming in and out of the main house often.

"We should pick up some beignets and coffee from Café du Monde for them. They'll need them after all that work."

Lucas smiled at me as he settled behind the wheel and pulled out of the parking space. "Your compassion has to be the sexiest thing about you, Flower."

My cheeks heated. "I'm a social worker. It comes with the territory. We can park on Decatur and walk over to Canal."

Lucas's smile vanished and a scowl took its place. "Are you sure you want to do this? We could pick up some beignets and go back to Willowberry without looking for a murderer. You realize we are likely dealing with a shifter here, right? You cannot stop one if they've gone rogue."

I cocked my head to the side. "You want me to ignore the images of a woman with her chest clawed open? They have haunted me all day. I *have* to do something. You say you like my compassion. Well, this is part of that. I am going to save this woman. That's why the fates have given me visions of the future."

His hands tightened on the steering wheel as he drove toward the French Quarter. Despite how much he hated the idea of taking me there, he was still doing it. That meant the world to me. I could appreciate his position and even understand it, but I refused to be stopped.

It was difficult to explain. The vision came with a sense of urgency, as well as a purpose. I knew it was up to me to save her life. And it kept pressing me, making it impossible to think about much else.

"Alright. But promise me you will stay with me. No running off if you see something."

A laugh escaped me, lightening the tension in the air. "As if I could outrun you. You're a wolf shifter. And not just any old werewolf. You're the alpha."

Lucas shot me a dark look. "We aren't werewolves. Those are constructs of Hollywood. But you make a good point. You wouldn't make it two feet before I stopped you."

"If I wanted to get away, I would find a way. Never underestimate a Smith woman. We have astounding powers."

He chuckled as he pulled into a parking lot on Decatur. "You're sexy when you get pissed."

I rolled my eyes and opened my door. The night was chilly, and I had forgotten to grab a jacket. It was colder as we got closer to the river. This could be a short excursion. Lucas came around the truck holding a brown leather jacket. He held it up with a raised eyebrow.

"Thank you. I didn't grab mine on my way out."

The leather smelled like him and enveloped me like a hug.

It was almost as if he surrounded me. I was learning how to tell when a scent would trigger a vision. Thankfully, there was no tingling at the base of my skull that preceded the dizziness and weak knees.

"Shall we head to Canal first?"

I nodded my head and twined my fingers with his when he reached for me. We walked hand in hand in silence for a bit. He allowed me to direct us when we reached the intersection.

"You said she had sandy brown hair?"

I scanned the people we passed. "Yes. It was difficult to tell how tall she was, but she had a slender build. He was dressed in black and big."

Most of those out were tourists carrying yards of margaritas. I tugged on Lucas's arm as we passed the spot where she would be dumped. My heart was in my throat. The scene was eerie at night, even though it was on a busy street with plenty of people going about at the moment.

That's because you've seen a dead body sitting there. Part of me wished I could give this power-up. I didn't want to see shit like this. I'd dealt with awful people who abused their kids for twenty years. I didn't need to see even worse stuff now.

Alright, pity party over with, I accepted the hand I was dealt and moved on in my mind. I needed to find a way to do something useful. Lucas nudged my shoulder. "Wanna get a coffee? We can sit at a table inside and people watch without standing here looking like creepers."

"That's a good idea," I agreed and we crossed the street and strode down to the coffee shop.

We entered and placed our orders, then took a seat at a table close to the window. Lucas moved his chair so his back was to the baristas and he was facing the window. I cradled the paper cup in my hands and watched the hotel across the street.

"This was a stupid idea. I doubt either one will be out here tonight." I felt like a fool all of a sudden. What were the chances they would appear before my vision became reality?

Lucas put a warm hand over mine and held my gaze. "I know I wasn't completely on board before. However, this is our only lead, so it makes sense to come here. You have keen senses, Flower."

"Thank you. It's easy to forget that when facing such steep odds." That only made me want to prove all the more that I could solve this regardless of it seeming hopeless.

"And yet, you don't let that stop you. I don't know anyone else that would even try. Your determination is admirable."

I snorted. "Dani would call it stubbornness."

"She's not entirely wrong," Lucas replied.

The strong scent of chocolate and cinnamon drifted toward me and that tingling started up. The vision came on me so fast, I was unsteady. Dizziness quickly followed, and I would have fallen if I weren't sitting on a chair.

I lost whatever else Lucas was saying as the coffee shop vanished and I was suddenly standing on one of the streets in the Quarter. There was no mistaking the Spanish style of architecture unique to the area.

I wondered if we were close to Final Swallow. It would make sense if those involved are paranormals. It was the first supernatural bar that discovered in the area. This vision likely had nothing to do with the murder. I wasn't in the same location.

The thought was depressing and made me scowl. I had hoped to learn more, but couldn't control these things. Could I? I focused on the dead woman as I looked around. A couple was making out a few feet away and others were walking along with their drinks in hand.

My vision wavered the more I focused on my victim. Before I knew it, I was standing on another street. I had no idea where I was. It could be anywhere in New Orleans. The Creole-style of homes with long layouts, steep roofs, and distinct porches started a few blocks from the Quarter.

My victim came walking down the street. I fell into step with her and thanked my lucky stars. I don't know what I did or how I was doing this. The image wavered the more I tried to figure it out, so I stopped and kept my attention on the victim. She had blue eyes and was a couple of inches taller than my five foot three inches.

Within a block, we turned onto Bourbon. I continued to follow behind her. Hoping to learn something more. I had no idea where she came from or what street we had been on. I hoped I could find it later.

My head swam, and my feet felt heavy. This was the longest I had ever been in a vision before. Refusing to leave, I kept my gaze intent on the victim. It paid off a second later when she lifted a hand and waved to a blonde-haired beefcake.

"Hey, Blade. How's it going?"

I never heard his response because I stumbled and felt like I was falling. My head hit Lucas's shoulder a second later. "Are you with me, Flower?"

"Yeah." My voice came out in a croak.

Lucas had moved his chair right up to mine and put an arm around me, no doubt saving me from falling off my chair. "You were gone for a long time. What did you see?"

I told him how I redirected the vision from whatever it was going to show me, along with what happened next. His forehead was furrowed. "Are you sure it was wise to derail the vision? What if it was something important?"

My heart dropped to my feet, and a lump settled in my stomach. "I hadn't thought of that before I did it. I won't be trying that again. Not only could I miss something important, but it took a lot out of me."

Lucas kissed the top of my head. "I know. You haven't lifted your head yet."

"Give me a minute, I will. Do you know anyone that goes by Blade?"

Lucas's shoulders lifted and lowered. "No. I have to admit that it's a relief to know the shifter isn't a member of my pack. I like to believe I have them under control, but I can never be too certain. And I can't afford to be blinded to the possibility. I will ask around, though."

"Thank you." I stayed like I was, watching the street as I digested what I'd done. I managed to direct my smell-o-vision and possibly missed something, but got information that might give us a real lead.

I could call it a complete waste of time and effort, yet I was ashamed of myself for having such a narrow focus without a care for what the universe was trying to show me. I made a vow never to do that again. Trying to see more of what I was shown was one thing. What I had just done was something different altogether, and I wasn't sure I was all that comfortable with it.

CHAPTER 8

❧

*D*anielle

I watched my sister pull the engraving off the CNC machine and compare it to the one she'd done on the laser engraver. "I like the layered shell from the laser better. The conch from the CNC might have more dimension, but with the five layers and designs, that one outshines it. Especially since I can see painting each layer a different color to give it more depth."

Lia stood back with me and put her hands on her hips. "I actually agree with you. And we can make it twice as big using the laser to create so many layers."

I grabbed a couple of bottles of spray paint and two of the layers. "Let's put a coat on each layer so she gets the idea when we take it to her. Cami, do you think you can use the heat gun to dry them while we print out the images of floral arrangements? I want to leave before rush hour starts."

Camilla grabbed the rest of the paint and heat gun. "That won't be a problem. I'm not afraid of it anymore. And I won't touch the end again, either."

Lia patted Cami's back and grabbed the other layers and

the single conch shell and we went to the barn where Steve had set up an area designed specifically for spray painting pieces. I loved it because before Willowberry, we were using old folding tables in someone's yard while contorting our bodies every which way to try and block the wind.

I might be out of shape, but thanks to the frequent painting I was limber. Something I was certain Noah would enjoy. *No, bad Dani. You aren't sleeping with the sexy wolf.* I wanted to grumble at my inner voice that I was an adult and perfectly capable of making my own decisions.

Seeing as I got out of a second failed marriage less than a year ago, I was listening. For now. "So where did you go last night, Lia?"

My sister swiveled around and the barn door smacked her in the ass. She hadn't thought I'd seen her leave. I knew she was on edge. I could hear her pacing in her bedroom for over an hour.

She sighed and shrugged her shoulders. "The Quarter with Lucas. Why?"

I narrowed my eyes. Normally, I would think she snuck off to make out with the hot shifter. However, the bags under her eyes would be less prominent and she would have a pep in her step if she had. "I saw you leave and was curious. Did you go back to try and have another vision?"

I knew Dahlia better than she understood herself at times. And it had been clear as day that she was carrying the responsibility for that woman's life. I knew from my work as a nurse how heavily such a burden was on a person.

Dahlia set her wood down and arranged the pieces on different tables. "No, I wasn't trying to have another vision. I was hoping either the shifter or the woman would be down there. I know it was silly to think I would run into her, so I could warn her. But it wasn't a total loss."

While I set the colors down by each layer, I listened to my

sister tell me what should have been an unbelievable story about how she managed to force one vision to focus on her victim.

Camilla was shaking a can of seafoam green spray paint as if her life depended on it. "How are you able to do such things? I didn't think you could control your powers."

Lia took the can from her and started spraying the board. "I have no idea. I remembered Phoebe and Kaitlyn saying that intent was key in magic, so I kept my focus on the victim and my intent to get more information to save her. It wasn't easy, and it drained me. Lucas practically had to carry me to the car. But it worked and I learned something."

I sprayed another board and Cami grabbed the heat gun while Lia moved to another piece. I wondered if I could do the same thing when I was sucked into the past. "I hope he and Noah find out who this Blade is so we save that woman." And we can put this behind us. No way would I tell her that. I didn't like how hard this was on her.

We quickly finished painting the pieces. Heat guns would speed the drying process. I glued the first three layers, then went to the house to print out images to take to Nedasea while Lia and Cami finished up.

The moment I exited the barn, I saw Noah walking toward me. My hand went to my hair and smoothed any flyaways down. "Hello, beautiful."

"Hi. What are you up to? I thought you guys finished up the roofs already." Noah and Lucas had been staples around the plantation for weeks while they worked on the roofs that needed repairing.

Steve was doing a lot of the interior work and even though he could use the help, we couldn't afford to hire them to do more. We'd spent the money Phoebe gave us on the kitchen and five other roofs we hadn't been aware needed repairing.

Thankfully, once Steve finished in the gift shop and we were done painting the rooms in the main house, we would be able to start adding tours and making more money.

Noah stopped less than a foot from me and tucked some hair behind my ear. "Lucas wanted to work on one of the back properties as a surprise for Lia. He's been collecting reclaimed hardwood flooring, and has a sink from another job he thinks will work well in one of them."

My face scrunched up as I continued walking and Noah fell into step with me. "What kind of sink are we talking about? We don't want to put just anything in these homes. With there being so many Airbnbs, we want them to have a warm and inviting atmosphere."

Noah chuckled and wrapped an arm around my waist, pulling me into his side. "I told him as much. He assured me you would like the copper farmhouse sink."

My heart skipped a beat. "Are you kidding? I want that in the main house for us! Tell him not to install it in one of those places. It'll be a while before we can get all the work done and rent them."

Noah opened the backdoor. "I'm way ahead of you, Sunshine."

Banging could be heard from down the hall. Lucas was under the kitchen sink when we stopped in the doorway. I hurried over to the copper beauty. "I absolutely love it. Thank you, Lucas. I won't yell at you for taking my sister to the Quarter and letting her do something so dangerous."

Noah quirked a brow at me. "Love, there is no stopping you from doing anything, and your sister is the same. Lucas did the responsible thing and kept her safe, as I would do for you. The Twisted Sisters aren't meant to be controlled. You guys are a force of nature. It's best to take a back seat and be there for support when needed."

My heart skipped a beat. That had always been a problem

for me. I refused to tolerate any semblance of control after my first husband. And I'd only grown more independent. For Noah to recognize that, and find a way to appreciate it showed what a unicorn he really was.

"I knew you two were smart. I need to print pictures then take them to Nedasea. Will you be here later?"

Noah cupped my cheeks and pressed his lips to mine. My toes curled as his tongue tangled briefly with mine. When he pulled away, I had to stop myself from yanking him back down for more.

"I will be here. Be careful when you're down there and call if you run into any trouble."

I nodded before floating out of the room with a ridiculous smile on my face. The office was next door, and I heard the ribbing Lucas gave Noah while I got what I needed.

Images and notes in hand, I hurried past the kitchen with a wave and met Dahlia as she and Camilla were exiting the barn. "Great timing," I told them. Lia and I jumped in her SUV and she drove us downtown.

On the way, I told her about Lucas bringing the copper sink and flooring. She tapped her fingers on the steering wheel as she drove. "How is it we find the perfect guys at a point in our lives when we are happily on our own and finally doing something we've wanted to for years?"

I shrugged my shoulders, having had the same thought many times over. "I've decided to stop questioning the fates or whoever put us on this path. I haven't liked many of the twists and turns, but I am happy where we are, so why risk messing that up?"

Dahlia pulled off the highway and into city traffic. Thankfully, we didn't have to go far before we parked. "Good point. I love the color choices on that shell, by the way. I wasn't sure how it would look with the various shades of beige and opalescence, but it works beautifully."

I glanced back at the conch shells that took up most of the back seat. "I wanted to bring out the seafoam in the top layers while also muting it so it didn't take over. Subtle is always your friend in these matters."

Lia snorted as she parked the car. "I learned from the neon lights blaring *I'm here*. Subtle isn't in my wheelhouse. I'm better off sticking to the heavy machinery and leaving the bows and color schemes to you."

I laughed at my sister. She and Dreya were the hardest working of us. Delphine was right up there with them. But Lia was right. Color combinations were not her strong suit. She could pick great ones when given specific choices, but she couldn't look at something and say put these together.

I was relieved when we made it down Canal without another vision. We did get a lot of strange looks as we carried the conch shells. Brezok was behind the bar when we entered and did a double-take when he saw us.

Nedasea squealed and clapped her hands as we walked into the dim bar. "Oh, my gods, you guys are amazing. I didn't expect anything so fast."

I tilted my head, scanning for a section with better lighting. It was difficult to see all the nuances in the layered shell where we were.

Dahlia set it down on the table and turned on the flashlight on her phone. "This isn't the best lighting, but you can get the main idea Dani was going for with this piece."

I leaned the CNC conch on the stool and grabbed the pictures from my shoulder bag. "We have two styles of shells to choose from for the large one you wanted. And, I have some ideas for flowers here, too. Don't focus as much on flowers right now as on style. I won't know what will be available at the mart before I pick them up. However, if there is something you have your heart set on, I will do my best."

Brezok came out from behind the bar and joined Neda. I

took the opportunity to scan the bar more thoroughly. Everyone aside from the fame demon standing next to me looked normal to me.

I noticed black and white images of New Orleans hanging on the wall this time that I had missed last time. They were clearly original prints and in great condition, considering. I wanted to get my hands on them. I made a mental note to approach Brezok another time about them.

Dahlia caught my eye and pointed to the images I was just admiring. Great minds think alike, fools seldom differ. I nodded my head eagerly, then refocused on our client. "What do you think?"

Nedasea picked up the layered one and held it above her head. "This is the one. The colors are perfect. Can you make it any bigger?"

Lia touched the side of the shell. "Our laser has a size limit of just under three feet, so I plan on cutting the image in half and using one-by to nail the halves together so it will be close to six feet tall. And I was thinking we could cut out your name and affix it to the middle of the shell. It would be yours to keep if you'd like."

We usually made something custom for each client and since Nedasea was so fond of the conch, we thought it would be something she would like."

Nedasea dabbed at the corner of one eye as if she were wiping away tears. "I would love that. This birthday marks an important milestone for a siren like me. This would make the perfect memento to mark the occasion."

I smiled at the siren while a million questions ran through my head. "Wonderful. And what about the flowers?"

We spent half an hour going over her choices and taking notes. Brezok went back behind the bar and had another waitress deliver drinks to us. Nedasea gave us the number of the restaurant that she had arranged to do the catering so we could liaise with them The siren left after that, and Lia and I finished our drinks. The fame demon made a mean pina rita.

I was a little tipsy as we gathered our stuff to leave. That was the only reason I didn't notice the guy until he was taking the conch from my arm and putting it back on the table. I gaped at him, wondering what the hell he was doing.

When I looked over at Dahlia, another guy had tossed her shell behind them and had his arms wrapped around her. She was pushing on his chest, but he wasn't listening.

"C'mon baby. Dance with me." A good-looking guy with dark hair, blue eyes, and a muscled body smiled at me. I didn't know who he was, and I couldn't tell what kind of supernatural he was. He looked like a normal human to me.

In another world, I might have found him attractive. However, there was something about him that made my skin crawl. There was no doubt in my mind this guy was a predator and he had me in his sights. Not a good feeling at all.

I grimaced and stepped back while pulling my cell from my pocket. He snatched the phone from my gloved hand and held it away from me. The bar had filled up while we were talking to the siren, and there were bodies everywhere now. My breath caught in my throat as my stomach roiled.

Panic surfaced, as I worried he would subdue me and drag me out of the bar to have his way with me. My heart raced while I looked around for a way out of this without causing a scene. "No, thank you. My sister and I are leaving now."

He chuckled and shook his head. "It doesn't look like she is going anywhere." The menace rolled off him in waves now.

I took several steps toward Dahlia, who was hitting the guy's shoulders. A muscular hand wrapped around my left arm and yanked me off course. I thrust my elbow back into his gut, making his breath rush out of his mouth. It smelled like potato salad left out in the sun.

"Leave me alone," I ground out. My legs were wobbly and every self-defense move I knew flew out of my head. I understood what a deer must feel like when caught in the headlights.

He scowled at me. "There's no reason to be like that." The desire in his voice was almost as bad as his rancid breath.

A grunt and curse sounded next to us and his friend was bent over while Lia glared down at him. Nedasea came running over and shoved the guy that had accosted me. "Jarek, you asshole. Leave her alone. You, too, Donovan. You both know better. Brezok works for these women, and if he sees you harassing them, he will ban you for life."

I wanted to run from the bar without looking back. Thank God for the siren. No one else in the bar was paying any attention to us. It seemed like they would have allowed these guys to accost us.

The men bared their teeth at Nedasea, who hissed back at them. I was too busy gaping at the fangs they were sporting to say much else. I should have known bloodsuckers existed. Honestly, it never occurred to me. My fear quadrupled in that second. I chastised myself, wondering if that was like chumming the water for sharks. The way Jarek leered at me said he enjoyed my terror.

The siren plucked the phone from Jarak's hand and gave it to me then picked up the layered conch and wiped it off. "C'mon. Let's get you guys out of here."

Lia took the shell and I grabbed the other one. "Will Brezok really ban them?"

Lia leaned close to us. "Forget that. Are they vampires?" My sister was shaking as much as I was at the moment.

Nedasea gave us an odd look. "Brezok tolerates their kind

because they tip well, but he looks for any excuse because they have a habit of harassing our customers."

Note to self, never come to Final Swallow alone. The mere thought that they were vampires was enough to make me demand Nedasea come to us. "Good to know. Thanks for helping us."

The siren shrugged. "You both would have likely been fine. It pissed me off when he tossed the conch aside like it was garbage."

Lia lifted one eyebrow in question. I shook my head and we said our goodbyes, then rushed out of the bar. Once outside, we walked as fast as our feet would carry us back to the car. I clutched the shell to my chest and kept a wary eye out. The sun had set, so those vampires might be able to follow us. Perhaps they could have during the day, too. I hated that our ignorance in the supernatural world put us in danger.

"I think that place was as bad as any regular nightclub." Lia said, breaking the silence. Her voice cracked and her shoulders were stiff.

Neither one of us had been partiers in our youth. We didn't frequent clubs when we were in college, either. We were both married and spent most of our time studying. I took a deep breath when I was sure they weren't behind us. "Next time I'm not drinking anything. I should know better that to let my senses get dulled. I've seen so many women come into the hospital after being roofied. Can you imagine what they would have done to us if they had incapacitated us?"

Lia nodded tersely. "They would have sucked the blood from our bodies. This world might not be all that different on the surface from the one where humans hang out. However, we are dealing with violent and aggressive creatures and we can't forget that."

My stomach roiled. "Perhaps we should talk to Noah and Lucas about how we can protect ourselves."

Lia's face darkened. "We don't need to ask them. Kaitlyn is coming soon. She can give us a charm or teach us a spell that will zap assholes like that if they try that kind shit again."

A smile spread across my face. I was finally starting to relax a little. "I like the way you think, sis. We're independent women and can take care of ourselves."

Lia nodded in agreement. "Not that we will relax our vigilance, but I agree that we won't drink when we go there. And no letting our guard down. I became complacent in there and that vamp took me by surprise."

"Me too. At least we know we've still got it. They were attracted to us with our flabby, saggy bodies." It amazed me that he hadn't been turned off when he hugged me close. There was no hiding my love handles the second he laid his hands on my hips.

Lia snorted. "We didn't need them coming onto us to tell us that. We have two hot shifters proving that to us on a daily basis."

"True that." And I wanted nothing more at that moment than to get home to Noah and cuddle up to a movie. Life had been crazy and chaotic lately, and I needed something normal.

CHAPTER 9

*D*ahlia
 My nerves jumped as I watched Kaitlyn walk up the path to the front door. No one ever used the formal entrance to the plantation. Lucas and Noah came in through the lower one that led to the port cochere and backdoor.

Thinking of Lucas sent a surge of guilt racing through me. I should have called him the day before and told him what happened at the bar. It made no sense why I felt that way. We weren't even in a relationship, yet I couldn't deny the urge.

I hadn't because I was still freaked out about being targeted by a vampire and he would pick up on that. I didn't want him and Noah searching for Jarek and Donovan because he was upset over their behavior. Lucas might be the official alpha, but they both had alpha tendencies.

"Why is she coming up the main path?"

I gasped and my hand flew to my chest as Deandra spoke over my shoulder. I'd been so caught up in my head that I hadn't heard her approach, which was ridiculous. We stood on the marble floor under the crystal chandelier that now sparkled brightly thanks to Phi's husband, Tucker.

The man had erected one of those platforms with plywood balanced between two sides. No one else wanted to climb the thing like Spiderman and lean over to clean the light fixture or reach up and paint the ceiling.

I shrugged my shoulders in response to Dea. "She's probably not used to people like us who bring you into the family and induct you to the crazy by putting you to work and feeding you."

Dea threw her head back and laughed, making me join in. By the time Kaitlyn knocked on the door, I had my legs clenched together to avoid peeing my pants. My bladder control was as weak as my son's excuse for not turning in his homework. Babies and age had a way of doing that to a person.

"Welcome, come in," Dea told the witch as she opened the door. We were still chuckling, and it said a lot about Kaitlyn that her lips lifted in a smile in response. "You don't have to come up the main walk. If you're going to be helping us with all this stuff, you're part of the family now."

Kaitlyn's smile widened and she inclined her head. "Let's see how you feel after we do some work together."

I waved my hand through the air. "There's nothing you could put us through that would be worse than Dani does before a party. Our events are so amazing because she's got a precise image in mind and makes sure we accomplish it exactly."

Dea started walking down the hall behind the main stairs, and we fell into step behind her. "It's true. Do you want anything to eat or drink before we get outside and get started?"

Dani and Dreya came out of the kitchen and waved when

they saw us. "Did I hear you telling Kaitlyn what a taskmaster I am?" Dani asked.

"She deserves to know what she's getting into," I replied, teasing my sister.

Dani nodded her head. "It's true. You should be aware. Especially when we throw the Beltane party in May. I will put you to work."

Kaitlyn shifted her gaze between the four of us. I swear I saw grief cross her expression, but it was gone too fast to say for sure. "Sounds good to me. I'd love to be an honorary member of the Twisted Sisters."

There was more there and I would ask her at some point. Right now, it was clear the high witch had no desire to discuss matters, given how quickly she shifted gears. "Are you guys ready to get to work? I want to run through some simple spells and see what happens. One of them is conjuring witch fire, so we should do this outside."

I cocked my head to the side. "I think you might have mentioned this, but what is the difference between witch fire and regular?"

Dakota and Delphine came out of the ladies' parlor and joined us. Phi held up her hand. "Witch fire is flames created from the individual's power. It is unique to them and can only be controlled by that person."

Kaitlyn beamed at Phi. "That's correct. You've been doing your homework. It is always unique in color, as well."

Dani scowled at Phi. "Where did you learn that?"

Phi shrugged her shoulders. "I read through one of Mary Alice's journals and it was in the back. There's a lot of information in those volumes."

Kaitlyn's expression brightened and became eager. "Did you happen to find her family grimoire? I would love to get a look at it if you did. Rumor is that her husband burned the volume in a fit of rage."

The mention of a grimoire piqued my interest. "Is that like a book of shadows?"

Dakota snorted. "Who's been watching too much television now? Real-life is not like it is on Charmed, even if Phi can freeze things like the middle sister."

Kaitlyn chuckled. "Actually, that show got a couple of things right. Every family keeps a book of shadows or grimoire. And we do use herbs and crystals in our potions. Spellcasting, though, is far simpler than a rhyming couplet, as you will soon discover."

Dreya rocked on her heels and shook her head. "I never thought this would be my life."

I headed for the door, eager to get to work. "Are you upset that it is, sis?" It would suck if Dre was unhappy with what had happened to us since purchasing Willowberry. We were the Six Twisted Sisters. It wouldn't be the same if one wanted to walk away.

There was a slight chill in the air when we emerged outside, and I considered going back for a sweatshirt. Recalling that Kaitlyn said this would be hard work, I opted not to. Being perimenopausal meant my temperature fluctuated at random. I didn't want to be stripping down while trying to do magic because a hot flash hit.

Dreya looked across at her house on the property and shrugged her shoulders. "No. I actually love being able to move things with my mind and hope to be able to do more. It's just a huge adjustment, is all."

Translation: Her hubby Steve was having a hard time. I didn't blame him after being attacked by zombies. He had to be terrified he couldn't protect his wife. Steve loved my sister to a degree I couldn't understand. He would adjust in time. Meanwhile, I made a mental note to give him some additional support.

Kaitlyn took over, leading us out into the back section of

our property toward the pixie mound and future rental units. She stopped in the middle of the field and turned to face us. She held her hands out at her sides. *"Revelare."*

Dani, Dea, and Dre stiffened. Dre stepped forward with her hands on her hips. "What are you trying to reveal?"

Kaitlyn's eyes widened at the venom in Dre's tone, and she backed up. "My intent is to reveal your true nature. Our goal is to discover what you are. We know you have Fae blood, but we do not know if you have more than that. I am inclined to believe that you do, in fact, have more. Fae rarely have some of the abilities you've shown."

I took a deep breath, trying to shake off the tension. "It has been an eventful couple of days. After this, we need to ask about putting up wards against the undead. We were attacked by zombies last night."

Dani crossed her arms over her chest. "Yeah, Marie..." I clamped my hand over her mouth and shook my head at my sister. Lucas had warned me about making unverified allegations against someone.

Dani scowled at me. Holding her gaze, I said, "We don't know who sent them. Of course, we have our suspicions, but we have no proof. We need to prevent a murder before we can investigate who is responsible, and we want to make sure they can't do that again."

Kaitlyn's expression darkened. "I understand your caution. While you can speak freely to me without worry, I do not recommend doing that with anyone you do not know very well. The consequences can be dire. But your wards should have prevented a zombie from crossing onto Willowberry."

"I hate to tell you this, but the spell you cast didn't work, Katy. This place was overrun with zombies. I had to conjure a couple of machetes and cut off heads," Dakota replied.

Kaitlyn pursed her lips and turned in a slow circle while

muttering an incantation under her breath. When she faced us again, her eyes were closed. "When did the pixies move to Willowberry?"

"Yesterday," I replied. "They helped us treat the wounds."

Kaitlyn's eyes were still closed, which made having a conversation with her a challenge. "They will be a boost to your plantation, and eventually, their power will naturally reinforce the wards. The zombies came from on your property. Whoever did this cast the spell from safety and used the dead buried here."

Bile filled the back of my throat, making me gag. Dakota shot me a wide-eyed look that told me she felt the same way. "There was at least one fresh zombie. What the actual hell?" Dakota's words echoed what the rest of us were thinking.

Kaitlyn's eyes flew open. "I cannot answer that one. But I can tell you there is nothing left here for a voodoo practitioner to exploit. Let's practice some magic."

It wasn't easy to shake off the thought. It became easier when Kaitlyn walked around and spread us out. "I want each of you to try and conjure witch fire. For this, *ignis* alone won't work. The proper chant is *ignis pythonissam?*"

Dre, Dani, and Dea had a leg up where spells were concerned because they were all registered nurses and had studied Latin in college.

"As with all magic, your intent here is key. Witch fire is specific to each practitioner and comes from her soul. You need to tap into the core of who you are when you think about creating your flames." Kaitlyn looked expectantly at us.

"You want us to do this now?" Dakota asked, when we remained silent for several seconds.

Kaitlyn's smile was patient. "Yes. I know this must be frightening. It's a simple spell and taught to witches before they hit puberty. They need to master it before their hormones get wacky."

Alright, I could do this. I took several deep breaths and let my eyes go unfocused. How the heck did I connect with my soul? I started by thinking about making a fireball in my hand, then tried to connect that intent to my body. I chanted the spell and watched, waiting to see the flames.

After the third try, I knew I was doing something wrong. Dakota's squeal brought my focus back to my sisters. Both of Kota's hands were engulfed in light pink flames. Her eyes grew wide, and she started waving her arms around. Flames dripped off and to the ground, where they quickly spread.

Kaitlyn shouted something before walking toward Dakota, as if she had all the time in the world. "Good job, Dakota. Now, I need you to calm down. The fire is reacting to your emotions. The calmer you are, the more control you will have. It will not burn anything if you don't want it to."

"Everything is on fire. Are you crazy?" Kota was growing more frantic.

Dreya turned to face Dakota. She was the only one that might get through to her. "You got this, Kota. Don't let the flames get away from you. You had four kids without any anesthesia. If you can do that, you can wrangle a tiny flame."

Dakota nodded her head and took a deep breath. The fire receded and went out a second later. Kota was smiling widely. "That was actually easy once I stopped panicking. You guys can do this."

I renewed my efforts to create flame as my sisters did the same thing. Sweat was pouring down my temples when, what felt like hours later, I finally managed to create fire. I honestly had no idea how I connected with my soul. I just imagined the power inside me like a glowing obelisk in the middle of my body and latched onto it.

Having seen Dakota's get out of hand, I maintained my cool and bounced the amber flames on my palm. "This is awesome."

Dani huffed and threw her hands up. "I can't do this. Can we try something else?"

Kaitlyn nodded her head. "Let's try casting a barrier to keep conversations private."

Phi tilted her head. "Like the silence bubble, Phoebe made the night she worked with the necromancer to get Camilla and Selene's souls?"

"Precisely," Kaitlyn replied. "Again, your intent is key when casting any spell. So, for this, you need to imagine a shield surrounding you that blocks all sound. The spell for it is, *secretum.*"

I recalled what Phoebe had done the night of the soul retrieval and kept that in mind while chanting the spell. The words echoed across the field for several minutes until Kaitlyn held up her hand, stopping us. "I believe Phi has managed to cast a barrier."

My gaze shifted to Phi, whose lips were moving, but no sound could be heard. Kaitlyn approached Phi. "To dismiss a spell like this, you can speak a dismissal, *dimitte.* Or you can alter your intent to have the spell end. The latter takes more time and experience to accomplish, so using the actual spell will be helpful in the meantime."

Kaitlyn spent the next several hours teaching us simple spells, like how to create an orb of light and a couple more complex spells, like how to locate something. There were mixed results, but each of us managed at least one enchantment.

Kaitlyn gestured to us. "It seems as if you six have more Fae in your blood than witchcraft, but you do have some, so I want you to think about setting up a sanctuary where you will keep your magical accouterments. It will also serve as a space for you to create potions and practice minor spells. I'd like to come back and go over potions another time."

I wiped the sweat dotting my forehead with the back of

my arm. "Is there some kind of formal training witches go through? This all seems so complex."

Kaitlyn shook her head from side to side. "No. Family members teach the young, which is something you six never had. That's why I will be taking it upon myself. It has come to my attention recently that I have been too hands-off in my role. I don't want a repeat of recent events and losses, so you've got me for a teacher."

"That's great. I would rather learn from you than anyone else. We trust you and know you aren't going to leave us in the lurch," Dani told the head witch. "Before you go, can we reinforce the wards around Willowberry?"

I lifted my hand. "And I have questions about sirens. We are planning a party for one, and we know nothing about her kind."

Kaitlyn gestured for us to come closer together. "Let's start with the protections. Join hands. I will draw from your power during the spell."

I clasped Dea's hand on one side, and Dre's on the other. The second we were all connected, a hum went through me. It was warm and vibrated my insides. It was such an odd sensation that I had a hard time focusing on what Kaitlyn was saying. We stood like that for several seconds before the high witch let Dakota and Dani's hands go.

Kaitlyn ran a hand through her hair. "Now, what do you want to know about sirens?" There were fine lines around her eyes that hadn't been there earlier. This time with us was taking its toll on her.

Before I could say we would talk later, Dani jumped in with questions. "Do sirens lure people to their deaths in the sea?"

"Sirens use their song to enchant victims and draw them, so they can take their energy. It's how they survive. Most sirens are dangerous creatures with no care for who they feed on." Kaitlyn's expression was grim, and it made my stomach knot up.

"Is there any way to protect against them? Should we cancel the party and refund Nedasea?" Phi's words came out so fast it was hard to follow her.

"There is a way to protect against the song. Magical earplugs are the key to blocking their lure. The correct chant is *impedimentum olfactus sanum* and you want to imagine those noise-canceling headphones covering your ears and not allowing the siren's song to get past them."

I was now uneasy about the idea of working with Nedasea. "Should we continue working with Nedasea? It seems risky."

"You are correct. It is dangerous. Even those sirens that live amongst the population have a hard time not giving in to their urges. That Nedasea not only lives amongst Mundies but also works at Final Swallow, and can reign her nature in means she is very strong. But there are rumors floating around that Nedasea was disabled and can't use her song anymore. I have never verified that and have never met the woman. If that is the case, then she poses no risk."

I thought of how she had intervened with the vampires the day before when they had selected Dani and me as their early evening meals. Nedasea didn't have to do that. Her reasoning might have been odd, but she cared, which seemed to go against what Kaitlyn was saying.

Dani nodded her head. "Thank you for your help. Next time we need to work on a vamp repelling amulet or spell. Oh, and we will have a space cleared out for our sanctuary before you come again."

"Can you send me a list of what we will need for the space? Herbs, crystals, candles. That kind of thing. I'd like to have the basics," Phi said.

"Will do. The vamp repellant might be difficult since

there isn't one in existence. Perhaps you guys can come up with one," Kaitkyn replied.

Crapo, that sucked. I was grateful for Phi and how she kept us organized. I doubt any of us had even considered stocking the space. My body was sore and I was exhausted. Kaitlyn had been right. Learning magic was hard work. Even harder than setting up for parties, which is not something I ever thought I would say.

CHAPTER 10

*D*anielle

The repetitive motion of running the flat tool down the wall was soothing. The morning had been eventful with having it confirmed that we were mixed Fae-witch and trying to learn magic.

To my surprise, casting spells didn't come naturally to me. I was used to being able to do anything I set my mind to with little effort. The measly yellow flames I managed were the exact shade of the sun, but no one's compared to the raging inferno Dakota had managed.

I paused and removed my gloves to dry the sweat that had pooled in them. Thanks to my wonderful ability, I had to wear them constantly, or I was sucked into memories when I touched anything.

The other night I went to the bathroom in the middle of the night and touched the toilet lid and saw Lia changing the roll while Mary Alice watched from the corner. Lia had been unaware of the ghost, so it didn't frighten her. Seeing it had given me the creeps and made me wonder how often the dead woman did that.

My head swiveled around the bedroom, searching for the spirit. Thankfully, she was nowhere to be seen. Camilla had gone to the post office with Dahlia to drop off orders from our Etsy page. When the ghoul wasn't around, Mary Alice was usually absent, which was what made seeing her creeping on Lia all the more disturbing.

I think the ghost would have liked to be the one teaching her daughter to read. I wondered how she felt about Cami joining us for magic lessons. She hadn't joined us with Kaitlyn earlier but we were rectifying that now. She still doubted that we wanted her to be involved.

I hoped the fact that we all came back and were eager to share what we learned proved to her she was wanted by us. I supposed it was difficult to erase centuries of believing no one cared whether you lived or died. I had no frame of reference to try and understand what she'd gone through. The events of her life that I'd seen didn't provide me with her emotional turmoil. Only the physical and verbal abuse.

Cami almost hadn't gone with Lia to the post office when she discovered the zombies came from the plantation. It bothered her to discover some of her friends and family had been used to attack us. Surprisingly she wasn't bothered that we had burned their remains. Instead, she prayed they had found some peace away from this place.

I was about to pick up my gloves when Mary Alice floated through the wall and stopped in front of me. She was gesturing wildly and talking rapidly. Her voice cut in and out, but I caught the end of what I think was a grimoire.

"Are you trying to tell me where to find your family grimoire? You need to slow down. I can't understand you."

The ghost nodded her head and flickered out. I stood there wondering if she was coming back for a couple of seconds, then gave up. I had one glove on when she popped back in. "You have to listen to me."

I jumped and dropped my other glove, then leveled the ghost with a glare. "You have got to warn us when you're going to shout at us and appear out of thin air."

"His power won't remain at bay for long. We have to hurry." Mary Alice flew to the wall and went right through it.

I rolled my eyes and walked out into the hall and checked the next room. She wasn't there, so I continued. When I reached the back stairs that lead to the third floor, I saw her hovering with an impatient air.

"Whose power are you talking about? Your husband?"

She shook her head from side to side and went through the ceiling. I climbed the wood stairs, praying whoever she was talking about wasn't hiding in any of our rooms. Cami picked a room next to Dahlia, and I went there first, but Mary Alice's ghost wasn't there.

I made my way to the other side of the attic where furniture was stored. The space had been cleared out, and we had put many of the pieces to use in the rooms, which made it possible to see to the other side of the attic.

Mary Alice was hovering beside the wall next to a chimney. There were actually several around the attic because fireplaces were how the house was heated centuries ago. I stopped next to her. "What do you need me to do?"

"The grimoire is behind the wall. You have to get it before he stops you."

I took a deep breath. "I have to grab tools to take down the wall." Steve was going to kill me because he would be the one to fix what I destroyed.

The spirit shook her head. "There's a hidden compartment. Push the third brick in the tenth row from the bottom to open the door."

I counted the bricks and reached out to push the one she mentioned. Not thinking, I touched it with my bare hand.

The musty attic was replaced with the smell of fresh-cut wood and stain.

"Who the hell are you?"

My head snapped around at the sound of the voice. A man with a thick white beard and black eyes was glaring at me. How the hell did he see me? When I went into the past, I saw what happened. I wasn't actually there.

"You can see me?"

"If you're here to get the book, you can forget about it. That witch's child will never get her hands on the knowledge. Mary Alice might have sealed it off from my reach, but I can stop anyone from getting it."

I opened my mouth to respond and pain arched through my grey matter, making me cry out instead. Clutching the sides of my skull, I braced my shoulder on the chimney to prevent myself from falling.

"You will never get back to help that bastard."

I couldn't think of anything beyond the pain and the need to breathe. The shooting pain radiated down my body and suddenly it felt like someone was stabbing me in a dozen places at once.

The malevolent energy I felt the moment the memory took me surrounded me. It clashed against mine which rose to protect me. I felt my energy pulse from my middle.

"That's not going to work, little witch."

"I'm not just a witch, asshole. I'm Fae, too." That meant something important. Too bad I couldn't form a coherent thought to find a way to get out of this mess.

The wind whipped my hair into my eyes, obscuring my view of the guy. It helped not to see the hatred in his black eyes. After a couple of seconds, I could recall Kaitlyn saying my witch fire would save us in impossible situations.

Desperate, I reached for that energy humming in my middle and called out for help. My body was suddenly too small to contain me. My hands dropped from my head when something shoved its way through my fingertips.

Through the tangle of my dirty blonde hair, I saw claws tipping the ends of my fingers. The glove I wore was shredded at the ends. My heart started racing as I wondered what the hell was happening to me. My skin hurt and I cried out at the discomfort.

The guy said something and instinct took over. My claws raked across his chest. His skin split and dark light poured from the wounds. I continued clawing at his body until the pain receded.

When I could see clearly, I noticed Mary Alice staring wide-eyed at me and the guy cowering in a ball on the floor next to the chimney. *"Ignis pythonissam."* Amber flames danced on my hands.

Footsteps echoed on the stairwell as I tossed the fire at the cowering mage. That was the title I had applied to him, anyway. He had magic and had used it to keep the family grimoire from being retrieved.

His scream hurt my ears and made me lose concentration. The tight feeling in my body vanished along with my claws. When my fire licked up the side wall, I focused on it, only hurting the mage.

Dahlia and Camilla came barreling into the room right before the mage vanished in a puff of acrid smoke. It smelled acidic, making me nauseous. "What the heck happened? And did I see claws on your fingers?" Lia stood there panting and clutching her side.

I lifted my hands and examined the shredded glove. "That was a mage that has been keeping Camilla's family grimoire from being found. Mary Alice told me it was safe to try and grab it."

I glared at the ghost in the room. She flickered and twisted her hands together. "It should have been. The wizard that cast the spell centuries ago tied his soul to it as a punishment for refusing him. I felt when he left the house."

Lia stopped beside me and looked at the scarred floor. "That has to be the guy Deandra has seen hanging around. Looks like you took care of him, sis. With some kind of claws, no less."

I shook my head. "I don't know what happened. He had me and was attacking magically. The only thing I could think to do was latch onto the magic inside me. That's when I grew claws." I didn't add that I felt like I was going to burst from my skin.

"They were dragon claws. Only a dragon's claws would be powerful enough to cut through his enchantment." The ghost's announcement left me speechless.

Lia didn't have the same problem. "Holy shit. We're part dragon. I wonder what that means for us."

"I have no idea, but Cami should get her book now. Kaitlyn said it might contain powerful potions and enchantments. We can talk about the claws when we are all here. Or maybe never. We don't even know what that might mean."

Dahlia pointed at me. "We will be talking about it. We will ask the pixies for a lead. They'll know who we can go to for information. In the meantime, I think you are right."

Camilla moved forward and stared warily at her mother. "Why are you trying to give this to me now? Why not when I was alive before and might have used it to save myself?"

Mary Alice's face fell. "When William hired Jonathan Williams to destroy the book, I knew I had to hide it. I couldn't simply give it to you. He would have discovered it and set fire to it. I put my own spell on it, prohibiting him from getting hold of it. That upset William and made him turn into a Dark witch. You know how things ended after that."

Camilla nodded and her mother instructed her on how to

retrieve the book. The hidden panel opened to a large storage closet. The book rested inside, along with a few crystals and a black cauldron.

The house groaned the second Cami touched the leather tome. She jerked her hand back and Lia picked it up for her. The move didn't stop the house's reaction. In fact, it shuddered and glass shattered somewhere downstairs.

"I hope that wasn't the glass in the front doors. It was original to the house," Dahlia said as she carried the book from the room.

Camilla gave her mom another look and left after her. I followed at a slower pace. That mage had torn me up. I might not be bleeding from my ears or have stab wounds, but I felt like I was inside.

Mary Alice floated along next to me. "Why won't she talk to me?"

I gaped at her. "Seriously? You allowed her to be abused and ultimately killed. That isn't something you just forget."

"I never had other children. She's my only one and I have so many regrets. All I want is to connect with her and for her to be happy."

I sighed and continued walking. "Your chance with Camilla has passed, Mary Alice. She has a chance for a new life. Your presence here is keeping her from truly putting her past behind her. If you really want what is best for her, you will cross to the other side."

Mary Alice's grief was so intense it weighed on me. "I would if I was able. However, Blood magic is keeping me here. I'm unable to leave the premises and cannot pass over."

My heart broke for the way this woman was suffering as well. She hadn't been the best mother, but it was clear she loved her child. And she had done the best she could at the time. I also needed to remember that she lived when women had no voice and no ability to defend their own wishes, let alone that of their children.

"I will look for a way to free you, I promise." I had no idea how I was going to help her. I had to help Lia find a guy named Blade before he killed an innocent woman. And throw a party for a siren.

* * *

NOAH ARRIVED when I was sweeping the glass from the big window pane in the men's lounge that had broken when the grimoire was uncovered. Camilla and Dahlia believed the house was reacting to having access to the magic.

Lia insists she felt something about the structure itself from the moment she set foot through the door. Before moving into the plantation mansion, I hadn't believed a word she said. Now, I knew magic existed, and that there was more to matters than met the eye.

Noah's smile was like the sun peeking through the clouds. "Hello, beautiful."

My face flushed, and I wanted to giggle like a schoolgirl. Who the hell was I right now? I wasn't a twenty-year-old woman that had never been burned by a guy before. I was a forty-two-year-old divorcee that knew better.

"Hello, handsome. What brings you by this afternoon?"

Noah closed the distance between us and swept me into his arms. At that moment I was that naïve twenty-year-old, eager to have more with the sexy shifter. Before meeting Noah, I had felt every year of my age.

When I was with my previous husbands, I was painfully aware of my flaws. Every extra pound was the elephant in the living room that we couldn't stop talking about. Hugo talked about my stretch marks and tried to get me to see a dermatologist about treatment for them.

He claimed it was because he read something about them potentially becoming dangerous for me. That had never been the case. He didn't like them. They were flaws, and he wanted the perfect trophy wife.

Shoving thoughts of my exes from my mind, I wrapped my arms around Noah's neck and kissed him back. His hold on my hips tightened, and he growled as his tongue tangled with mine. It vibrated through my mouth, making me wonder what that would feel like when he was kissing other, more intimate areas of my body.

I was so aroused I thought I might combust when he pulled away from me and rested his forehead against mine. "Sorry, you are so damn sexy. I couldn't help myself. How are the party plans coming?"

I sighed and forced my naughty mind to banish every naked image. "Coming along. She finalized the decor and flower and we have several of the decorations cut out of the laser and waiting to be painted. We're doing everything by phone now to avoid the assholes at Final Swallow."

Noah's body stiffened beneath my hands and he held me at arm's length. "What happened?"

Oops. Lia and I had discussed keeping the incident with the vampires to ourselves to avoid upsetting the guys. No avoiding it now. "A couple of vamps hit on us and refused to take no for an answer. Don't worry, we put them in their place and Nedasea backed us up."

Noah's nostrils flared, and his eyes narrowed. "I want to know which vampires. I will make sure they know never to mess with you again."

I ran my hands down his arms. "There is no need for you to do that. We handled it. They won't be bothering us again. But if I get worried about them hunting us down, you are the first person I will go to."

Noah's nod was jerky and clearly forced. "I want you to

hire bodyguards for your events. You and your sisters are attractive women and do these events on your own. You should have capable individuals around in case you run into problems."

I was shaking my head back and forth. "We have been fine for years. Now that we have our own venue, we have even more control. Don't overreact because of a couple of bloodsuckers."

"This request is not about the vampires. I have considered it since the first time Marie Laveau came to visit. You aren't dealing with mundies anymore, Sunshine. Paranormals are stronger and faster. You never know what might happen during one of your parties. You six are just learning about yourselves. I worry about you guys."

"Speaking of getting to know our heritage. I believe we are at least part dragon. At least that's what we think the claws I grew earlier mean. But I will consider your request. It would be nice not to leave that to Steve. He can't do much in this world."

Noah's jaw had dropped to his chest. His mouth opened and closed several times, making me wince. "I suppose that's a deal-breaker for you."

He cupped my cheeks and looked into my eyes. "Not in the least. I'm surprised, is all. I should have picked up on that. Are you able to wield spells like a witch?"

I nodded my head. "We each managed to conjure our witch fire. Mine is the color of the sun. I'm not very good at it yet."

Noah wrapped both arms behind my back and held my torso to his. "You will get better. I'm surprised you can partially shift like that. Usually, when a hybrid shows abilities of both races, they have aspects of their animal but can't shift any body parts."

My lips lifted. "That's because I'm amazing. New territory, remember?"

Noah chuckled. "I will find suitable bouncers for Nedasea's party if that is alright with you. We can talk more about that later. Right now, I want to know if you will have dinner with me tonight."

He was smooth, sneaking that bit about bouncers in there, then asking me out. It worked too, because I nodded my head eagerly. "I'd love to. Give me a couple of hours to get this grime off me and I will be ready."

He pressed his lips to mine briefly, then let go of me. "It's a date. I will be back to pick you up in a few."

I followed him as he walked out of the room and watched as he walked down the hall. He filled out a pair of jeans and then some. Damn, he was good-looking. When he was gone, I hurried up the stairs to look for an outfit that could perform a miracle and transform me.

Where was a fairy godmother when you needed one?

CHAPTER 11

Dahlia

Camilla dried and put the last plate from dinner away. I dried my hands and hung the towel. I needed the ghoul to go to bed so I could take off, but I didn't want to hurt her feelings.

Ever since we found Dani fighting some ghostly wizard over her family grimoire, she had been more withdrawn. "Are you alright?" Southern manners had been drilled into me and they demanded I make sure she was good before taking off.

Cami shrugged her shoulders. "I'm alright. I can't stop thinking about what Mary Alice said. Do you really think she wanted to give the book to me?"

Camilla was vulnerable right now. She wanted to believe her mother cared more than she ever knew before, but was afraid to let herself. If she learned later that it had been a lie, she would be devastated.

"I think that your mother did everything she could for you. It is clear how much she loves you. If it were me, I would do the same thing to protect my daughter. It would kill me if I ignored the danger and gave her something that brought about her demise." I had skirted around the issue, yet I could see my answer helped her.

She smiled at me and cocked her head to the side. "I think if I ever had kids, I would feel the same way."

"Do you want to look through the book? I can read it to you, or help you read it." I was an awful person for silently wishing she would decline my offer. An image of the dead woman popped into my head, making me ignore the guilt.

There was a person's life riding on me finding Blade. I wasn't going to do that sitting around the house. Dani was out on a date with Noah, so tonight was the perfect night to look around. I wouldn't confront anyone, I just wanted to see if I could find that street the woman had been walking down. Ideally, I would run into her.

Camilla chewed on her lower lip and glanced out the window above the sink. "I don't think I'm ready for that. I'd like some time to practice more spells first."

"Are you concerned because you haven't conjured your witch fire yet?"

She shrugged her shoulders. "Maybe, I don't know."

I shook my head at her. "We talked about this, remember? You're a witch again. We need to talk to Kaitlyn and ask what it means that you used to be a ghoul. Whatever she says, I guarantee that it isn't because you aren't worthy of the magic. I've never met a person more deserving."

Cami's face brightened, and to my surprise, she hugged me tightly. "Thank you, Lia. I don't know what I would do without you guys. You have all been so wonderful."

I started walking out of the kitchen, hoping to speed the end of the evening along. "We are the ones that have been blessed by you. There are no other plantations that can say they have an original resident to tell the stories. Not that we will let anyone know that about you. Just that you are special and can give the guests a unique experience."

Cami was back to chewing on her lip as we walked down the hall. "I'm glad we have some time. I promise to keep practicing so I don't let you down."

"There is no reason to worry. You just be yourself and tell them what the rooms used to be used for, how they were heated, and how the bathtub used to be filled. Add in a few stories to make it interesting and you will have them hooked."

She smiled that time and nodded her head. "I can do that. Speaking of baths, can I go take one?"

I chuckled and patted her shoulder. "You never have to ask permission. There are fifteen bathrooms in this house. Use one of them and take your time. I'm going to read a bit, then head to bed."

My gut churned over my white lie as Cami left me at the library. I waited until I heard her footsteps on the stairs before I made a beeline for the mudroom by the backdoor. We'd converted part of the laundry room into a space to discard wet shoes and coats. It was where Dani and I kept our keys and purses when we were home.

Leaving my purse on the hook, I grabbed my ID and a credit card along with my keys and cell phone. Stuffing them in a jacket pocket, I headed out the door and locked it before heading to my car. We started locking it at night after the zombie attack. Better to be safe than sorry. Especially with Camilla being left home alone.

Dreya and Steve are across the yard if she needs them. The reassurances fell flat as I got in my car and took off toward the Quarter. My heart raced as if I'd just committed a felony. I was not cut out for a life of crime. Good thing I was on the other side of the law.

I parked in a lot I was familiar with rather, than trying to get closer to the street I thought the woman had come from. My focus needed to be on finding her or the guy, not where I parked my vehicle.

The cost to park downtown was ridiculous. I handed the attendant my credit card and found a spot. Within minutes I was walking down Canal toward Bourbon. Halfway between the two, I wondered if I should call Lucas.

The night was warmer than usual for February and there were a lot of people out and about. That made me feel a lot safer. I was less likely to run into any problems with all the tourists walking around. Right?

Taking a deep breath, I continued until I reached Chartres and turned down the smaller street. It would be easier to reach the end without being swallowed up in the chaos of Bourbon. That was where most of the action typically was on the Quarter.

The downside of that was the number of pedestrians walking on Chartres was reduced by half, though there were still a good number of people. I held my breath as I walked past a couple smoking cigarettes. I wasn't trying to avoid a vision, just the noxious fumes.

I made it four blocks and paused as I considered where to go from there. I'm not sure why I was so worried. No one had given me a second look. I would be able to find the street and look around, then get home without anyone knowing I was gone.

I might be antsy and feel guilty for lying to Camilla, but it was a relief to be actively doing something. I couldn't explain why I felt this incredible sense of urgency about this woman. I just did, and it was driving me insane.

I thought the woman came off Ursuline or St. Philip. I'd lifted my foot to head in that direction when a hand wrapped around my mouth while a large arm wound around my waist. The arm was covered in fur.

My scream was muffled. Nausea rose to choke me as I got a smell of sour milk right before my back hit a hard body. I would rather have been hit by a truck than be in some strange man's hold.

My mind whirled as panic took over and my fight instinct kicked into high gear. I kicked and wiggled and tried to bite the hand over my mouth. My efforts earned me a wrenching of the neck that made me worry he was going to snap my neck. Those thoughts all raced through my mind in a fraction of a second.

"Stop fighting it, little witch. It's no use."

How did this asshole know I was part witch? I needed to get away from him, but I couldn't move with my arms pinned at my side like they were. My cockiness was going to be my undoing.

Why had I been so stupid to think I could come down here and get home unscathed? The lights of the street grew smaller as he dragged me further down the alley.

There was no courtyard in sight. Only dumpsters with rotting food and grimy brick walls. When the area narrowed, I pulled my knees up to my body and kicked off the wall.

Only one of my feet hit the wall, but it was enough to make the guy hit the opposite wall. He lost his hold on me and I fell to the ground. I landed in a heap and crawled toward the street a few feet away.

Something nasty squished beneath my hand, sending the smell of rotten fruit wafting to my nose. I gagged as I kept moving. I would bathe in dog poop to get away from this guy.

I didn't make it very far before fingers latched onto my white-blonde hair. The asshole yanked hairs I couldn't afford to lose from my scalp, making it sting. He lifted me into the air and snarled at me.

The sour milk smell compounded the bile playing at the

back of my throat. Through watery eyes, I noted the guy's dark brown hair. It was almost black. His eyes were like a shark's. There was no life there at all and they were pitch black.

I kicked out and scratched the arm holding me up. He bared sharp teeth and sprayed me with toxic spit. My face stung, and tears blinded me, which was probably better because he threw me through the air a second later.

My back collided with the dumpster. Something in my chest cracked. Breathing felt like hot knives were cutting through my lungs. *Had to have been a rib.* This time, I could put my hands out and break my fall as I dropped forward onto the concrete.

"Why are you doing this? Please let me go. My sisters will come looking for me. So will my boyfriend. He's an alpha wolf. You don't want to mess with him."

Instead of intimidating him, this guy threw his head back and laughed. It infuriated me and also gave me a chance to get a better look at him. His clothes were pristine. In fact, they were one designer label or another, if I wasn't mistaken. Why did he smell like he hadn't showered for a decade then?

I hated to admit it, but I assumed he was homeless. His entire demeanor screamed cold-blooded. This was the guy that killed the woman in my vision. Only, it wasn't. Blade had blonde hair and broader shoulders than this guy.

He was lunging for me and I lifted my arm over my face and my leg in the air. I also tried to force claws to come out of my fingers like they had Dani's earlier. It would help if I could claw him to death and get away.

He twisted my arm and batted my leg away. The pain that ricocheted through those limbs joined the fire in my chest. "I like the smell of your magic, little bird. I'm going to enjoy draining you."

I tried to conjure my witch fire. Unfortunately, that didn't

113

work. He was toying with me now. I shut out his taunts and braced for the punches he would throw. It was difficult to think straight, so I didn't bother trying to cast a spell anymore.

Taking a full breath became impossible, and my heart stopped racing. It was now laboring to keep a regular rhythm. I was going to die down here at the hands of a madman.

God damn, I had screwed up royally. This entire excursion of mine went all kinds of sideways and now my sisters would lose me. I would never know what might happen with Lucas, either. Worst of all, my kids would become orphans.

No! You are not giving up. Magic isn't the only way to fight back, Lia. Use your head. What had that self-defense teacher taught me all those years ago? Go for the groin, eyes, instep, and nose. The only area I had a shot at reaching was the groin.

I curled into a ball, pretending I was taking the abuse. He wasn't using his full strength, so I had hoped nothing else was broken. There came a point when I couldn't tell because everything hurt like a bitch.

When he got closer and inhaled deeply to smell me, I kicked out with all my might. My aim was good and my foot crushed his twig and berries. I refused to wonder if he was aroused or not.

His bellow was accompanied by my scream for help. I had little hope of being heard or found, but I was going to damn well try. The guy's eyes were red this time when he came at me.

Spittle was flying from his mouth and he gripped my arm and leg so tight I swore he cut through every layer of skin and muscle. My body tensed as much as it could before he hurled me at the wall.

My lower back bounced off the steel ladder of a fire

escape right before the rest of me hit the wall behind it. I couldn't lift my hands fast enough and my chin impacted the ground.

My vision was blurry, but I know I saw someone standing at the mouth of the alley. "Help me, please. He's killing me."

The guy grabbed my hair right as a dark light filled the alley. It lit up his enraged features and the grime I was lying in. I didn't give a shit as long as I survived. That was what antibiotics were for.

Blood trickled down my head and into my eyes. I lost sight of the person heading this way and brought my arms up over my head, expecting the guy to end it now. Instead, the rattle of metal told me he was making his escape.

It took all my energy, but I turned my head and watched him disappear. What little breath I had left me in a rush and I tried to sit up. I couldn't move. My side hurt as bad as my chest did now. My legs weren't much better.

The face of a woman I recognized hovered above me. "Dahlia? Is that you?"

I squinted to make sure I was seeing the long brown hair and light blue eyes correctly. "Yes," I croaked. I was in pretty bad shape. No way was I getting home on my own.

I wasn't entirely sure I would survive this now that my unlikely rescuer, Temperance, was there. The last time I saw her, she was working with Marie Laveau to take over the ritual for the ghouls.

"I was never working with Marie. The necromancers hate her, and thanks to Phoebe, her hold over us is crumbling. She might be the Queen of the Dead, but she no longer tells me what to do." The fierce conviction in her voice instantly made me like the necromancer.

How had she heard my thoughts? Could she read my mind? "Did I say that out... loud?"

"Yes, you did. Don't worry about that. Right now, we need to get you some help."

My next breath was sheer agony. "Can you call Dani on my phone? She'll know what to do."

Tempe lifted one eyebrow. "I think we need a hospital first."

"Dani, please." I was growing weaker. And I was so cold. My body started shaking, increasing my discomfort. If I was going to die, as we had been for our mom, I wanted my sisters with me.

Temperance said something else, but my ears weren't working. The last thing I saw before my eyes slipped closed was her talking on a phone. Good, Dani would bring the others. They would be here soon.

CHAPTER 12

Danielle

My heart was lodged in my throat by six-inch white-hot nails and I couldn't breathe. I stopped and ran a hand over my face. I wanted to throw up, then rush down the hall and demand privileges back so I could get the inside scoop on Dahlia.

I swear my world came to a halt when I got the call from Temperance. It took me back to the day my mom called and told me she was seeing a doctor for a rash on her breast. It turned out to be inflammatory breast cancer, and we lost her a little over two years later.

We were not going to lose Lia. We couldn't. She was one of my ride-or-die people. I broke out in a cold sweat just thinking about it.

"What the hell was she thinking?" Deandra was pacing with me and not using her privileges to get information. Knowing her the way I did, she was too afraid of getting bad news and having to be the one to share it with us.

Dakota scowled at Dea. "What she was thinking was that we were doing shit to help her find this woman and save her life. She saw something horrific that hasn't happened yet and we have been telling her we will do our best to find the woman. In reality, we haven't done crap."

Dreya sighed and nodded her head. "Kota's right. I haven't felt any urgency because I don't have pictures in my head, keeping me up at night, haunting my every waking hour. However, you can bet if I had seen what she had, then I would do anything to help."

Guilt froze me in my tracks alongside Dea. They were right. If I was honest with myself, I had hoped she would forget the mission. I'd been incredulous when she even suggested we investigate the crime. We weren't detectives or patrol officers. We were freaking party planners. None of us had the skill set to investigate crimes.

"I ignored her," I admitted. "I hoped our lack of experience with solving crimes would stop her from pursuing the woman."

Noah's eyes widened, making me feel like I was a complete asshole. We had been close to the hospital thanks to the date we had been on. "You six are incredible women, but you are clinging to your previous lives. You aren't those people anymore. You have new roles and need to adapt and change with the demands they bring."

Lucas huffed and stood up. He was a big guy, and it was clear at the moment he was pissed. "Lia didn't trust any of us to help her. We have all failed her and I will not allow that to happen again. If she doesn't make it, I will make it my mission to find Blade and eliminate him myself."

The powerful alpha's voice cracked as he mentioned the possibility of Lia not surviving. This guy really cared for my sister. Their attraction was obvious and so much fun to watch. I wanted Lia to hear how much Lucas cared. It would probably freak her out and make her happy at the same time.

Deandra's shoulders started shaking. "I've been so

consumed over trying to function day to day while seeing ghosts everywhere around me, I ignored her plight. I won't do that again. I will help you find him, Lucas. Of all of us, I should have known it would upset her. I know how difficult it is to see the dead and I don't see how they passed away."

Phi rubbed her arms like she was trying to start a fire with them. "We need to focus on sending her energy. If we can help her survive until the doctors fix whatever is wrong, then that's what we should do and where we should pour our energy."

Temperance stood up and headed toward the open doors of the surgical waiting room. Thankfully, there were no other families in here at the moment. "Delphine has the best idea. You need to focus on helping your sister right now. I will get out of your hair."

"Wait," Dreya called out. "Please stay, Tempe. I know Lia will want to thank you for helping her. And we owe you more than we can say. We would have lost her for sure if you hadn't come along."

Lucas turned to the necromancer. "How did you end up there, anyway? Weren't you giving tours?"

Temperance looked from Lucas to Dreya. "My mom was the only one that ever called me Tempe. I like hearing it again. It highlights my new freedom from Laveau. To answer your question, Lucas, I have no idea what drew me down that street. I had just finished up my nightly tour and was heading home, which is in the opposite direction. I didn't question it and I am so glad. Although she might not thank me for calling an ambulance before you guys. She tried to insist I call you, Dani and I almost did. I'm not familiar with mundie emergency services, but I knew she was badly injured and to call nine-one-one."

"Why would she want you to call me and not an ambulance? I couldn't have saved her." It made no sense. I was in no way capable of saving a person on death's door and Dahlia knew that.

Noah stood behind me and squeezed my shoulders. "Do you think she could be afraid of having her magic discovered?"

The first thing that popped into my head with his question was the Salem Witch Trials. Not a good moment in our country's history. If people knew witches were real, I could easily imagine much worse happening today. Such as becoming a test subject in some medical lab.

I shrugged my shoulders. "I have no idea. It wouldn't be my first thought."

"I bet she was frightened and knew how badly she was injured. When mom died, she said she hoped she was surrounded by all of us when it was her time." Dreya's words made those six-inch nails squeeze around the heart in my throat all over again.

"What did you see when you heard Lia's cries for help?" Lucas's voice was a growl and made the necromancer flinch. Camilla burrowed closer to Dakota as well.

To her credit, Temperance hid any fear she felt. "At first, I passed the alley without noticing anything. The sound of something big hitting the fire escape brought me back. If my hearing wasn't as acute as it was, I might not have heard anything. When I reached the mouth of the passage, I saw shadows. Two steps down the narrow opening and I saw someone fly into the wall. Dahlia's cry for help pierced my heart and stunned me for a second. I don't know how she saw me, but she did and my surprise at coming across the attack froze me. Thankfully, my appearance was enough for the attacker to see me and run. The guy jumped onto the metal ladder and scrambled away."

"Did you see his features? Given the search she was on, it's possible she found Blade and confronted him. Any detail will help because if it wasn't the asshole from Lia's vision, then I have two to kill." Lucas didn't bat an eye over talking about murdering someone. Then again, I was silently cheering him on. I wanted this guy to pay for hurting my sister.

Tempe shook her head from side to side. "I didn't get a good look at him because it was dark. My vision allowed me to catch his dark hair and not much else. I considered going after him, but refused to leave Dahlia. I was afraid she would die."

Lucas's eyes seemed almost hollow as he stared at the necromancer. "He wasn't blond? Was he a big guy? Broad shoulders?"

A thought occurred to me. "Was she close to death? Is that something your powers allow you to see?"

Temperance chewed on her bottom lip. "Yes, I can sense when someone is close to death. There's this tingling in my gut right before the spirit leaves the body. No, this guy was not a big guy and his hair was dark, almost black, I would say."

I sucked in a deep breath and leaned against Noah for support as I asked my next question. "Did Lia's condition trigger your sixth sense?"

Tempe's expression was filled with remorse and sadness. "Yes. It's why I didn't bother calling you first. I knew time was of the essence. Whatever led me to that alley wanted her to survive. I tethered her soul to her body, hoping to buy the doctor some time. Once the spirit leaves, it is nearly impossible to save the person."

Lucas growled and punched a hole in the wall. Noah left me to go to his alpha and get him under control. Tears filled my eyes and the ache in my chest intensified. I hated waiting.

Deandra must have felt the same way because she announced she was going to get some answers. Before she made it across the room, Doctor Carassco entered the room.

Dea, Dre, and I rushed to his side. "How is she?" Dea demanded. She was the only one still working at the hospital, so we let her speak for us. I didn't think I could form words at the moment, anyway. Emotion was choking me, and I was barely holding back my tears.

The doctor took a deep breath and put his hands on Dea's upper arms. "Your sister is alive. She's in rough shape and has a long way before she's out of the woods, but she is still with us."

Dea nodded, and her tears broke free to run down her cheeks. "What are her injuries?"

Doctor Carassco looked around the room and shrank back when his gaze landed on Lucas. The alpha was pissed and looked ready to rip the physician's head off. I gave Noah a look, asking for help. The last thing we needed was a terrified doctor. He was Lia's chance to live.

Noah said something under his breath to Lucas, making him back off. I turned back to Carassco, who took a deep breath. "First, she suffered an acute subdural hematoma, as well as injuries to her spleen and liver. We drilled burr holes and are draining the bleeding, but the severity will more than likely result in brain damage. We were forced to remove her spleen and are monitoring the liver lacerations. If it doesn't subside soon, we will have to go back in and perform a lobectomy."

The tears I had been holding back flowed down my cheeks. Dahlia would never be the same. I'd seen people lose the ability to talk or feed themselves after injuries like this. She might be alive, but she wasn't going to be the same sister.

Her survival is all that matters. You can feed her if you have to. I would do anything for her. We thanked the doctor and headed to her room. To my surprise, Temperance followed behind us.

We entered the room, and Lucas fell to his knees at Dahlia's side. Boy, this guy had it bad for her. Not that I blamed him. Even the necromancer crowded the bedside with everyone else where Lia lay.

Her face was battered and bruised like a ten-day-old peach. Cuts along her arms and chin were stitched and there was a bandage wrapped around her head with a tube coming out of the top.

Lucas pressed his forehead to Lia's hand, and I noticed even they hadn't been spared in her attack. They were both cut up, as well. The hum and beeping of the machines were as familiar to me as breathing, yet not comforting. Dahlia's stats were awful.

Lucas stood up and gently held Lia's hand while his entire body shook. "I didn't understand much of what the doctor said, except she lost her spleen. What does this mean for her?"

Deandra had her hand on Dahlia's foot. "It means she still might not make it and if she does, she will not be the same person she was before. Parts of her brain have been destroyed. If you have a subdural hematoma, your prognosis depends on your age, the severity of your head injury, and how quickly you received treatment. Lia's was as bad as it can get, but thanks to Tempe, she got help quickly."

"About fifty percent of people with large acute hematomas survive, so her chances are good as long as the liver stops bleeding," Dreya added. "She might not be able to perform basic tasks, her personality could be different, and she might not be able to speak at all. I've had more than one patient that was loving and kind become an abusive jerk after a head injury like this. Their impulse control is also gone, along with their ability to make good decisions."

"What?" Lucas wobbled on his feet and I worried he might actually pass out. He held Lia's hand more tightly now.

Noah stood next to his alpha while shifting his attention between Lucas and me. I saw the debate going through his mind. He wasn't sure who to help. I nodded to him, trying to assure him he should stay with Lucas. I had my sisters to hold me up if I needed it.

"She is going to live," I promised Lucas. "We won't let her die. The rest is up to the fates. They've given us so many blessings since we started on this path and I am letting it be known that we would trade them all to have her whole and healthy."

I had no idea if the elusive fates were listening or not, but I was putting that out there. I would take out a loan to pay Phoebe back her money and give up anything else I had to in order to help Lia.

"I can't lose her now when I just found her," Lucas replied. He brushed a finger over the gauze on her forehead. "What can we do to save her?"

Temperance cleared her throat and looked around at us all. "You're witches, right?"

The five of us nodded our heads. "Part-witches," I clarified. "But we have no idea how to heal her."

"Or if it's even possible," Dakota added.

"You don't have to know. As residents of New Orleans, you fall under Kaitlyn's purview, so you can reach out to her for help."

Dreya's head lifted, and her eyes were narrowed. "What kind of help? Is it possible to heal her?"

The necromancer held up her hands and took a step back. The boulder in my gut got heavier. "I have no idea if a healer can do anything for your sister. I don't know enough about that kind of magic, but I do know they healed Stella when she was on death's door after a vampire attack."

My heart skipped a beat. "Call Kaitlyn!" I didn't mean to shout and make my sisters jump, but we needed to get help here, now. The longer Dahlia lingered in this state, the more likely she would suffer brain damage.

Dreya pulled out her phone and dialed the head witch. Temperance tried to slip out of the door when Dre told Kaitlyn what had happened. Dakota grabbed Tempe's arm and wound hers through it. The necromancer had a tear in her eye, making me wonder how long she had been on her own.

I hadn't trusted her after the previous ritual. Now, I owed her more than I could ever repay. She'd put herself at risk to help Dahlia when she was being attacked and hadn't hesitated to do what was needed. That made her a good person in my book.

Dreya smiled when she hung up the phone. "Kaitlyn said there is a healer not far from here and she will bring her to the hospital within the hour."

I squeezed Dahlia's leg gently. "You hear that, sestra? Help is coming, just hang in there and everything will be alright."

For the first time since Temperance had called me on Lia's phone, my heart dropped back into place and I took a deep breath. The ache in my chest was still acute, but my sister was going to live. And might avoid lasting damage.

I sent a silent thank you to the fates for listening to my plea. I doubted I would ever truly get used to how the magical world worked. If only we had these powers when mama was sick, we might have been able to save her, too.

Noah left Lucas and came to my side, then wrapped me in his arms. I hugged him back and settled in to wait for our miracle to arrive.

CHAPTER 13

*D*anielle

My stomach was in knots, and my heart ached. Every second that passed, I knew Lia was suffering more and more brain damage. The hematoma was draining, but the intracranial pressure was still much too high for my comfort. Dreya and Deandra also understood what the probe was telling us.

Lucas's skin went from fur-covered to caramel-colored flesh every couple of seconds. He was as agitated as a long-tailed cat in a room full of rocking chairs. His growls filled the room, yet he never left Dahlia's side or let go of her hand.

Phi stood up from the chair next to Lia's bed and gestured for me to take a seat. Normally, the Neuro-ICU only allowed two visitors inside each room. They needed to allow space for quick reactions in the event of an emergency. Not to mention keeping the atmosphere calm for the other patients. One of the perks of having worked there for over a decade and still having a family member employed at the hospital was they made exceptions for us.

"I can't sit right now. How long is it going to take them to get here?" It seemed like it had been an hour since Dreya had talked to the head witch.

Dakota crossed the room and sank into the chair, rubbing her knee. "They have to get here soon. How long can she last? I want Lia to get back as much as she can. She has had such a hard life. She doesn't deserve this, too."

"You're right about that, sis. But I talked to Kaitlyn less than fifteen minutes ago," Dre clarified. "They will be here any minute. What I want to know is how we can locate the guy that did this to her."

Lucas finally lifted his head and snarled. "As soon as I know Lia is out of the woods, I will be going out hunting for the guy. He will regret ever touching her."

Temperance sighed from the corner of the room, drawing everyone's attention. Lucas scowled at the necromancer. "Did you catch anything that might help lead us to him?" Lucas's voice was sharp and made me flinch, but Tempe didn't show one hint of being affected by it.

The necromancer moved closer to the bed. "There was something odd about him. He didn't feel like any creature I'm familiar with. It was almost as if it was in this world, but not. It triggered my death magic, but not in a way that made me think he straddled the line between the living and the dead."

"That doesn't sound good," Phi observed. "What kind of supernatural would trigger you without being dead or connected to death somehow?"

Dea's forehead furrowed. "Is it a type of demon? They seem intimately connected to death because they kill and cause mayhem. At least according to Phoebe and Aidoneus."

"Demons typically have a distinct scent of brimstone, so I will be able to follow it if it is, in fact, one of them. However, it would have to be a Lord of the Underworld. Lesser demonic entities would not be able to transform and appear human." Lucas had turned his gaze back to Dahlia. It was as if he was compelled to keep his eyes on her.

Noah moved away from Lucas and leaned against the wall next to me. His closeness eased some of the tension churning in my gut. I smiled gratefully at him and twined my fingers with his when he reached for me.

"Should we call Teagan, Eli, and Mack? They're a few hours away at college, but they should probably be here with their mom." I know how much Lia loved her kids. They became her entire world after she lost Leo.

Kota rubbed her temples with a grimace. "Honestly, I'm not sure. What do we tell them? That she was attacked by some unknown magical monster. Oh, and that she has this weird smell-o-vision? I can't imagine they'd take that well."

Dakota had a point. None of us had told our kids about magic, yet. Kota's husband knew because she'd been wishing for things the second she got home. Deandra told her husband, Maleko, but Phi had yet to tell Todd. Steve knew because he lived here and there was no way to hide it from him.

"Let's hold off on calling them for now," Dreya advised. "We can revisit the idea after we have more answers." I knew she was thinking of saving them if Lia didn't remember her kids. It would devastate them if that happened.

Lucas's head shot up and his nostrils flared as he faced the door. Beside me, Noah had a similar reaction. My heart started pounding, and I searched for a weapon. "What is it? Are we in danger?" We could try to cast a protection spell around Lia. Our magic wasn't consistent yet, but together we might be able to manage something. No way would we leave her so vulnerable.

Noah's hand tightened around mine. "There's no danger. Kaitlyn and the healer are here."

My breath rushed out of me at the same time the door

opened to admit two women. One was familiar to us. Kaitlyn's long black hair was in a ponytail on the crown of her head. Her tight jeans revealed a backside that reminded me of Kim Kardashian's butt.

"We got here as soon as we could. This is the coven healer, Kip. How is Dahlia?" Kaitlyn headed right for the bed as she spoke.

I was focused on the woman behind her while Dreya introduced us and told them the pressure on her brain was still concerning and that Lia hadn't shown any signs of waking up yet.

The short black woman that Kaitlyn had introduced as Kip paused in the doorway. "Do you know if she was hurt by magical means?" She was in her late thirties with black hair and light green eyes. The combination was stunning. Her voluptuous figure only added to her beauty.

I released Noah's hand and stepped forward. "Temperance discovered Dahlia while she was being attacked. I'll let her tell you what she witnessed and her impressions, but from my understanding, Lia's injuries are consistent with being beaten and battered."

Kip's eyes went wide when I gestured to the necromancer. Tempe ignored the healer's reaction and gave her and Kaitlyn a rundown of what had happened and her thoughts.

"It's a good thing no magic was detected. Otherwise, I might not be able to help her. Physical ailments and injuries are relatively easy to heal. But once they are inflicted using powers not so much. I would need to know the power source in order to eliminate it." Kip's voice had a Cajun accent similar to how our parents talked, only the healer's was thicker.

Kip had a warm energy that radiated from her. It immediately made me feel better. "Tempe told us you healed

Phoebe's friend when she was on death's door. Do you think you can save our sister?" I chewed my lip after blurting the question out. It would not help to shout at her and shake her violently.

Dea held up a finger. "And keep her brain from being permanently damaged? That's the most important thing right now."

Kip entered the room, allowing the door to shut behind her. She stopped next to the bed and lifted a hand over Lia's head. "I can help your sister. But only because Temperance was there to call for help. If the doctors had not done the hardest part of the job by relieving the pressure on her brain, the cells would be beyond my ability to rejuvenate. Because much of the swelling is down, I can ensure the cells that suffered injury don't die off from lack of oxygen, which, as you may know, causes the actual brain damage."

I sagged against Noah and let him hold me up. The night had been one roller coaster ride of emotions. The ups and downs made me sick to my stomach and left me disoriented and dizzy. Or maybe that was from the worry over her situation.

Kip pointed to the tray table that was pushed against the wall closest to the bathroom. "I'm going to need that to prepare the potion."

Phi was close and brought it over to the bed. Kaitlyn pulled a black tablecloth from the brown leather bag over her shoulder before she set it down next to Lia's legs. Kip joined the head witch and began withdrawing jars and setting them on the table. They smelled like herbs and incense.

"She suffered a severe head injury. Do you know who attacked her? Or why? I am not picking up any anger, which I would have expected. More annoyance and avarice, which makes no sense. The damage she endured speaks of rage or a supernatural predator."

Kaitlyn shivered and wrapped her arms around her waist. "I pray there is not a monster preying on witches. We cannot lose another member of the coven. It would devastate us all."

Dea crossed her arms over her chest. "Lia is our sister. *We* would be crushed."

The head witch nodded. "You are correct. It doesn't matter if the others do not know Dahlia. They will still be impacted if she dies."

I cocked an eyebrow. "Why's that?"

Kaitlyn took a deep breath. "Because you are now connected to us all. A coven feeds and lifts one another up. It's why many seek to keep members separate from each other. We are formidable when joined physically."

I nodded. "Will it make this process easier for you, Kip, if we add to your efforts?" Emotion choked me. I would do anything necessary to help Dahlia recover and come out of this intact.

Kip was standing by Lucas, close to Lia's bandaged head. She placed her hand over the gauze. "I am uncertain if I will need you five or not. It depends on how well her cells react to my ministrations."

I moved closer, as did Dre, Dea, and Phi. Dakota stood up and placed her hands on Dahlia's leg. Warm energy flowed from Kip. It reminded me of plants and gardening, only there was more. I had no reference for the effervescent quality I sensed in Kip, so I couldn't place it.

"I'm just assessing her for now. Testing the waters, so to speak," Kip informed us.

"Thank you, Kip. We owe you more than we can ever repay."

Kip shook her head from side to side as she turned to grab a bottle of something that was placed on the table.

131

"There is no reason to thank me. It is my job as the coven healer. I can seal the wound to her scalp completely and replace the blood she lost during surgery. If we join powers, your sister will have a better chance at a full recovery. Some of her brain cells already feel dead, and I doubt I can do much for them on my own. Duplicating cellular structure to replace what is lost takes more than I have on my own."

"We will do whatever it takes to help Dahlia." I would battle demons for her. So would the others.

"Tell us how to help," Dreya asked.

"Join hands with each other and Kip. Open your energy to her. You will have the urge to throw her from your power when you feel her latch on. Don't act on it. Think of your sister and imagine it's her taking from you when the drain becomes pronounced." Kaitlyn's instructions seemed easy enough.

"Thank you for warning us. I might have conjured a knife and stabbed someone," Dakota replied. "I'm still jumpy after the zombies attacked the other night."

Dea winced. "Any ideas on how to open up? I have no idea what that even means."

Kaitlyn chuckled while Kip mixed some herbs together and instructed Lucas to remove the gauze from Dahlia's head. "Magic users have a natural barrier up around their power that you need to lower or open. Think of your energy being contained in the center of your body behind a door. To open up and allow Kip access to your resources, all you need to do is twist the knob and push it open."

I followed Kaitlyn's instructions. The second my door opened, I felt Kip latch onto my power. It felt like someone had taken hold of my chest and began pulling. It made my heart race and my breathing turned erratic.

It wasn't so bad. There was no urge to force her out. I fought tears as I caught a glimpse of Dahlia's shaved head and the staples keeping her flesh shut around the shunt. Kip was spreading a mixture on her scalp when pain stole my ability to breathe at all and made my eyes go blurry.

Shit, Kaitlyn had been right. Thanks to her warning, I resisted the urge to slam the door in her face. My lungs relaxed by increments, saving me from brain damage in the process. My vision cleared and I could see the bruising around the injury shift through the healing phases.

The knowledge that Kip was taking from me and giving it to Dahlia warmed me and eliminated the worst of my discomfort. A nasty scent filled the air. It was a cross between disinfectant, mint, and old blood.

My eyes watered when Dahlia stirred. She didn't open her eyes, but her head turned toward my side of the bed. Next to me, Delphine laughed out loud. The sound was watery, indicating she was crying. "It's working. She's waking up."

"She's going to be alright," Dakota exclaimed.

Lia winced and groaned. "Keep it down, will ya?"

I had no words for the relief that flooded me at that moment. I'd hoped this would work, but in the back of my head, I kept warning myself not to get my hopes up. It hadn't been that long since we discovered magic was real. Never in a million years would I have believed it would be capable of saving my sister after an injury like this. I knew the reality of an acute subdural hematoma.

"Holy shit," Dakota muttered.

Lucas bent and pressed his lips to Lia's forehead gently, then brushed a bit of the paste on her scalp away. "You scared us, Flower. How are you feeling? Do you remember what happened to you?"

Dahlia moaned, and her head moved in the opposite direction slowly. My heart was back to pounding in my chest. She didn't seem completely healed, after all. My mind immediately went into triage mode.

Her coloring was improved, but still pale. The bruising around her injury was no longer deep purple, but lightening. She was breathing on her own, still, which was another positive sign.

A glance at the monitors told me her heart rate and blood pressure were going up. The intracranial pressure reading made my heart skip several beats. It was no longer in the danger zone. It was practically normal.

Dahlia's eyes moved behind her lids but didn't open. "Am I alive? Since I didn't see a bright light or mama waiting for me, I hope that means I'm not dead."

A laugh escaped me. It was clear most of her brain was functioning like normal. "You are alive and in the hospital. You had brain surgery."

"Do you recall what happened?" Lucas asked again.

I shot him a scowl. Why was he making her think of her attack? Kip grabbed a cloth and rubbed the paste away, revealing an unhealed surgical incision around the drain tube. What was better was the swelling beneath the skin. If that area was that much better then her brain must be a lot better.

"It's important to know what you recall," Kip told Dahlia.

One eye finally blinked open and focused on the healer. The other followed, and both eyes were pointing in the same direction and seemed to be moving together. "Who are you?"

Kip smiled at Dahlia, set the cloth aside, then placed her hands over her chest. "My name is Kip and I'm the coven healer. Your sisters called Kaitlyn, who enlisted my help in saving you. Now, what can you tell us?"

Lia winced when her eyebrows drew together. "I was searching for someone. A woman maybe. I can't recall."

The draw on my energy disappeared, so I let go of Phi

and Kota's hands, then lifted Lia's hand into mine. "Were you looking for the woman from your vision?"

Her gaze shifted my way, and the wrinkles around her eyes vanished. "Yes. I couldn't wait any longer, hoping for a miracle to drop into my lap. I *have* to keep her murder from occurring."

Kip pursed her full lips and shook her head. "I appreciate your fervor and dedication to saving a woman's life, but you cannot walk around the Quarter by yourself. It's dangerous."

Lucas leaned close to Lia's face and cupped one of her cheeks. "You just about killed me, Flower. Promise me you will not do something so reckless again. I will be there anytime you want to follow up on a lead."

Dahlia's eyes filled with tears and she cried out as she nodded her head. I panicked and rounded on Kip. "Did you heal her or not?"

Kip placed a hand on my arm. Her warm energy suffused me, calming my anger. Was she an empath, too? "I healed the brain swelling and restored the damaged or dead cells. But she still suffered significant abuse."

Temperance stepped forward and squeezed one of Lia's feet. "Speaking of your attack. I am glad to see you're awake and alert. I was worried about you."

Lia focused on the necromancer. "You saved me." From the furrow of her forehead, Lia was recalling details as she spoke. "The guy would have killed me if you hadn't arrived. Thank you."

Lucas growled low in his throat, and fur sprouted on his arm, making Lia flinch. Dre jumped in between the pair. "What did you do to her? If you hurt her, I will shove that IV pole up your ass."

Dahlia tried to lift a hand and gasped again. "No. It's not him. The guy that did this had furry arms and black eyes that turned red when he was mad."

Lucas inhaled and let it out slowly. His body was shaking. I could see the effort he was expending to keep his anger under control. It was also obvious that he wasn't mad at Dahlia or any of us.

Lucas shifted around Dreya. "What else do you remember?"

"He smelled like sour milk and garbage and wore designer clothes. At first, I swore he was the guy from my vision except he had greasy black hair and was smaller than the killer I saw." Lia tried to sit up but Kip wouldn't let her.

The healer shook her head from side to side. "Stay put. You've got broken ribs and a fracture to your skull, as well as bone bruising in several places. I cannot heal too much or the doctors will become suspicious. I've already done too much, but I had no choice. If I'd done any less, you would have been left with severe deficits."

My stomach soured when I heard that. Dahlia's face went ashen and her lower lip trembled. "I knew it was bad. That's why I tried to get Tempe to call you guys. I didn't want to die alone. I wanted you guys with me."

A howl left Lucas loud enough to rattle the windows. "I am never leaving your side again." His vow was a complete surprise, yet it wasn't. It was clear the guy cared about Lia deeply.

Lia smiled at him and turned her hand over, then wiggled her fingers. "You cannot be with me twenty-four-seven. You have a job and so do I. I am going to be alright thanks to Kip. Knowing I have your support is reassuring and eases some of the pressure I feel pressing on me."

I patted Lucas on the back. "Don't worry. Dahlia's attack changes the way we will approach most things. We've already agreed to your bouncers at events. And none of us will be venturing places alone, night or day. Especially when we will be encountering paranormals."

Dakota nodded in agreement. "Dani's right about that. I'm not sure I can go to the store alone anymore."

"Changing the subject completely, I need to have a game plan to give the doctors about why Dahlia healed so quickly." Deandra nudged Kaitlyn out of the way and grabbed fresh gauze to wrap around her head like it was before.

Kip helped hold Lia's shoulders while Dea worked. "I left the skull fracture, so you have a weak spot that will cave if you suffer another blow. The swelling can be explained by the drain they inserted above the hematoma."

Temperance cleared her throat. "We can say she avoided permanent damage thanks to my quick reaction. I told the ambulance that I called the moment I saw the guy pick her up, so they think the time-lapse was less than thirty minutes before surgery."

The lump in my throat shrunk. "We can work with this. We've seen miraculous things in the past. If she still has the fractures, few eyebrows will be raised."

Deandra taped the gauze in place. "The healed skin beneath the sutures is harder to explain, but I will run interference with the busybodies."

I tugged Kip into an embrace, then moved to Kaitlyn. "Thank you both. Let us know how we can repay you for helping her."

Kip and Kaitlyn shared a look before the head witch focused on me. "What do you know about the Wiccan holidays?"

I thought about her question and realized my knowledge was limited. "I know about Samhain and Beltane. At least the information contained in paranormal romance books. I have no idea about the accuracy of what I've read. Why?"

Kaitlyn's smile was stiff. "We would love for you to host the Ostara or Samhain celebration. Willowberry is perfect for the bonfire and celebration." It was interesting that she didn't mention Beltane. I definitely needed to follow up with her on that.

Dakota patted Kaitlyn on the shoulder. "For what you guys have done for Lia, we will host every celebration from here on out."

My eyes went wide and my jaw went slack. I was flabbergasted by her offer until I considered what they had given us. I closed my mouth and nodded in agreement, along with Dea, Phi, and Dre. "It would be our pleasure. We will get dates from you and block them out of the calendar."

"We will need information about rituals and themes, so we don't plan something garish," Phi added.

"I had planned on teaching you about witchcraft and its history, along with ceremonies and important dates. We will have other coven members assist with the events. This will give you a chance to get to know the other witches as well." Kaitlyn gathered up supplies from the table and stowed them in the leather bag.

Kip nodded her head. "Many are excited to have so many new powers added to our ranks, as well as party planners. They'll be excited to hear we can add amateur detectives with powerful friends to the list. We have needed someone to investigate incidents for a while now."

I sighed and dropped my head. I didn't want to be a detective. I would have gone into law enforcement if I had. One look at Lia and my frustration melted away. Our powers came with responsibilities and I wasn't going to ignore them ever again.

Fate had proved her point to me. She had plans for us and if we weren't in it together, we would lose each other. I would do everything I could to prevent that from happening. I didn't have to ask the others to know they were on board with that notion.

CHAPTER 14

Dahlia

My mind was swirling, and I didn't follow much of what my sisters were talking about with the visitors. I hadn't expected to wake up after that assault. The pain I experienced during the attack, coupled with the inability to lift my hand, told me I was in bad shape.

The last thing I remember was Temperance coming to my rescue and scaring my attacker off. I was convinced he was the one responsible for the murder in my vision, which made no sense.

Perhaps I didn't come out of this completely unscathed. What had Dani mentioned about brain cells? Or had it been Deandra? I couldn't remember. My head was still foggy and I hurt everywhere.

Warmth spread through my chest and made me drowsy. Glancing down, I saw a pair of black hands with long fingers. My eyes lifted to a beautiful black woman who was smiling down at me. Who was she? She was the witch that had healed me.

"Thank you for helping me. I owe you more than I can

afford at the moment. Do you have a need for personalized gifts?"

Lucas brushed a finger across my cheek, drawing my gaze his way. "Dani was just talking about hosting the coven's celebrations as a type of repayment. Do you remember that?" His grey eyes looked like a stormy afternoon. It was impossible to miss the depth of his concern.

I took a breath and choked when a searing pain stabbed through my chest. The coughing only increased the discomfort. "I wasn't paying attention. I'm still processing that I'm not dead when I was so certain I would never see any of you again."

Lucas leaned down and pressed his forehead to mine and took a deep breath. "You are allowed to ignore the rest of us. I'm glad you no longer smell of death." He pressed a light kiss to my lips and straightened.

Dakota jerked and scowled. "She smelled like death before? Did you notice that too?" The last question was directed to Tempe.

The necromancer nodded her head. "Her lifeforce teetered on the line between the living and the dead. It is one reason I stuck around so long. I wanted to do what I could to ensure she survived."

Dani wrapped an arm around Temperance's shoulder. "Without you, she wouldn't have survived. I've become a big believer in the fates and decisions they've made about our lives. I no longer question if our path was meant to cross yours."

Tempe chuckled. "I never would have expected a bunch of mundies turned witches to believe in the Moirai. Few supernaturals do anymore, which I think pisses them off."

A toddler hopped up on sugar had better focus than I did at the moment, but I thought I was following the conversation. "We're new to the magical world, but I can't imagine not believing they exist and have a hand in things. I mean ,what are the chances of you happening to walk by at the exact moment I was being attacked?"

Tempe shrugged her shoulders. "There was definitely more at play. I was heading in the opposite direction when I was forced to reroute by a strange urge. There was power behind it. I have no idea if you have a powerful guardian angel or the Moirai foresaw this event and moved pieces so we would cross paths at Willowberry, then again tonight. Why were you out there alone?"

I winced. "As I said before, I couldn't ignore the vision of the woman. It was stupid, I know."

The necromancer shook her head. "You mentioned that you felt compelled. Given our discussion of the Fates, do you think you had to go through this? That something was driving you to go on this excursion alone? It's clear to me that any of your five sisters would be more than happy to have gone with you, yet you didn't ask."

"I would have taken you," Lucas interjected.

I tried to rub the ache in my chest. Unfortunately, my hand flopped like a fish onto my stomach and never made it that far. "Honestly, I'm not certain about that. If the Moirai did indeed set me up to be attacked, I'm not as positive they are nice entities. I almost died, for crap's sake. What would be the benefit of having me suffer like this?"

Kaitlyn smoothed the end of the blanket over my legs without paying attention to what she was doing. Her focus was on me. "This incident has set the Twisted Sisters up as an official investigative team. None of you took these powers seriously or thought they could have been given to you for a reason. What Dahlia has gone through changes all of that? You have a new ally in Temperance and you've ingrained yourselves in the coven. Both things will help as you face different challenges in the future."

Dani's eyes flew open, and she gasped. "Are you saying we're some twisted version of Nancy Drew? I never liked those books as a kid. I'm not cut out for this."

A new ache in my chest blossomed, joining the searing pain. "You don't have to help me. I'll find this woman and Blade without you. I would never ask you to do something you don't want to, sis."

Dreya placed a hand on Dani's shoulder. "This is precisely what got us in trouble, to begin with. None of us gave Lia's vision the attention it deserved and, as a result, she went out on her own. I think Kaitlyn's right. Our life is different now."

Dakota ran a hand down her face. "How the hell are we supposed to adjust when we have no idea what will be thrown at us?"

"We roll with the punches and make changes as necessary. There are six of us, so when Lia gets a vision, or something else happens, we won't have to drop clients. This is the first time this has happened since we got the powers. It might not always be so bad," Deandra added.

Delphine squeezed my toes. "Dea's right. There is no reason to fret over something we aren't even sure will be a big part of our lives. But you, Dahlia, will never be going out on your own again. If Dani can't or doesn't want to join you, call one of us."

Dani rolled her eyes. "I will always have your back. I just don't want anyone in this room spreading rumors that paranormals should come to us if they have a problem. Phoebe mentioned something about being so busy with stuff she hadn't been able to throw her daughter a birthday party. Our livelihood is all about throwing parties. We have to make enough money to eat and pay the bills."

"Oh," Camilla exclaimed. "You could always charge for your investigative services if people come to you and you take a case. That would be another revenue stream, right, Phi?"

Delphine beamed at Cami. "Yes, it would. And, it's not a bad idea. However, with Dea and I still working full-time elsewhere, we need to stick to addressing Lia's visions when she has them."

Kaitlyn held up a hand. "You also have a coven you can turn to for help. How can we assist in this pursuit?"

Noah nodded his head from behind Dani. "You have the shifters as well. And I suspect that Phoebe would help if needed. For a family with less than three months in the magical world, you are already surrounded by powerful friends."

I hadn't thought of that before. "I have no idea how you can help unless you know anyone named Blade. That's what the woman with dirty blonde hair called her attacker."

"Is she a paranormal?" The healer's question threw me for a loop.

I'd been so focused on the killer being a shifter of some kind that I hadn't wondered if she was a member of the magical world or not. It was entirely possible she was a mundie.

"I have no idea. I don't get much information in the visions. Initially, all I saw was his back and her dead body. I know he is a shifter of some kind because of the claw marks on her torso. The one time I could redirect my vision and see her before she was dead provided no information about her except that she was heading to the Quarter from one of the neighborhoods nearby."

Kip pursed her lips and shrugged her shoulders. "I don't know a shifter by that name. As for the woman, it could be one of the thousands in this city. There isn't anything to go by based on what you have now. It would help if we had something more."

I rolled my eyes and was rewarded with a renewed pounding in my brain. "That's why I was out there tonight. I had hoped I could find the street and induce another vision, or run across her. Anything that would give us an avenue to investigate."

Dani taped the rail at the end of the bed with her fingers. "Where was she headed in that last vision? Did you see the name of a restaurant or bar or anything?"

I shook my head once, then stopped. "There was a grey building behind her, but I can't be sure if it was a house or business. We need a list of paranormal businesses that we can visit."

Lucas scowled at me. "Are you thinking of trying to trigger your smell-o-vision again? It drains you when you do that."

I met his steely gaze. "What choice do we have?"

Lucas was saved from responding by a knock at the door. The panel opened and an attractive man stepped into the room. "You're awake. That's good news. How are you feeling?"

"Like I've been tossed against a building several times." I read the name on his white lab coat. It said Dr. Carrasco, MD FACS.

The doctor approached the bed and pulled a penlight from his pocket. "The police will be by in the morning to speak with you. I need to do an assessment to see how the swelling is doing and how you are recovering. I have to say, I didn't expect you to be awake."

Deandra chuckled. "Us Smith girls are tough cookies."

Dr. Carrasco smiled. "I'll say. If we can have some privacy, I won't take long."

I lifted my hand off my stomach. "They can stay unless you're going to undress me."

One of the doctor's eyebrows lifted to his hairline. "I

don't need to remove your clothing."

He went right into his assessment. He had me do several things, such as keeping my head still but following his finger with my eyes, and touching my nose then his finger. His questions were designed to see if my memory was intact. I knew he was doing a neurological assessment and cooperated despite the pain some of it caused.

When he was done, he shook his head. "I'm not sure how you are doing so well. You should be unconscious with far more fluid still on your brain. I expected you to come out of this with deficits. I don't understand it."

Deandra's laugh was forced and completely unlike her. "I've never known you to doubt your surgical skills. You did an excellent job like always. It helps that Tempe saw the attack happen and got her help right away."

Dr. Carrasco nodded. "Your quick reaction saved Lia's life and functioning. You still have some swelling and several broken bones, so, unfortunately, you will be in the hospital for another couple of days until the drain can come out. I'll be back to check on you later."

"That was way too close for comfort," Dea said as the door shut.

I groaned as my way of agreeing. The exam had taken a lot out of me and made the pain nearly unbearable. Dea moved around the healer and Kaitlyn and approached the monitor and IV stand.

"I'm increasing your morphine drip. You didn't need as much when you were unconscious."

"Thanks, Dea." I forgot what I was about to say when I saw Temperance twisting the doorknob.

"Wait, Tempe. I have a question. Did you notice anything odd about the guy that attacked me? I swear he had fur and scales, but that could have been the head injury."

Temperance shook her head. "I didn't notice much. He

felt odd to me, but I couldn't place why. He was definitely magical and connected to death somehow. Other than that, I have no other information. Sorry."

I sighed. "It's alright. I swear he felt like the killer from my vision. I know it sounds crazy. He was much too small and had dark hair."

The necromancer's lips twisted to one side. "He didn't feel like a shifter to me."

I nodded. "I wasn't in the best of shape. It had to be my imagination getting away from me. Thank you again. Let's have lunch sometime."

Temperance agreed, then said her goodbyes. My eyes started to slide closed as Kip and Kaitlyn took their leave. I tried to stay awake and talk to my sisters, but I couldn't keep my eyes open. I'd talk to them later.

✎

CHAPTER 15

*D*anielle
"Go have fun, sis. You don't have to stay here with me all night again. If I had a hot shifter asking me to go out to dinner with him, I would jump at the chance." Lia looked and sounded much better than she had last night.

The room had been crowded as the Twisted Sisters all stayed, as did Lucas and Noah. No one wanted to leave her side for fear she would take a turn for the worse. I hated seeing her covered in bruises. I couldn't wait until she was discharged so Kip could come to the house and heal the rest of her.

Lucas waggled his eyebrows at Lia. "You do have a sexy shifter asking you on a date, Flower. All you need to do is get better and I'm taking you to Atchafalaya. You like Cajun food, right?"

Lia's smile and the way her eyes lit up almost made me forget the bruises covering most of her right cheek. "The first thing my mother fed me as a baby was red beans and rice. I'd love to join you, but I won't be presentable for a bit."

Lucas stood up and bent to kiss Dahlia. It was brief, yet

the passion between them lit the room. Cami got up and cleared off the tray table at the end of the bed. Camilla was uncomfortable with most displays of affection. She'd admitted to Lia and me a couple of weeks ago that she had never kissed anyone. My heart broke that the only love she had known in her short life had been from her father before he was taken from her.

"You are gorgeous, Flower. However, I'd feel better if I brought you dinner and you continued to rest and recover at home." Lucas sat and clasped Lia's hand in one of his.

Noah nudged my shoulder. "Your sister is in good hands. The others have gone home. Camilla and Lucas can handle anything that might arise."

Lia scowled at me. "I should be going home tomorrow. They removed the drain a few minutes ago. There is nothing that can go wrong that the doctors and nurses can't handle."

Rolling my eyes, I squeezed Dahlia's foot. "You're right. I'm worrying for no reason. I will be back tomorrow to pick you up. Are you alright staying here, Cami?"

Camilla tossed an empty cup in the trash can. "Yes. I'd prefer to stay here rather than be at the house alone. Have a good time. We will be here when you return."

I gave Cami a one-armed hug and waved to Lia and Lucas. I paused at the nurse's station and let them know Lucas and Cami were staying and to call me if anything changed.

Noah twined his fingers with my leather-covered ones. "You carry too much on your shoulders. You are the only sister that has refused to leave her side."

I grimaced and sucked in a breath. He had a point. "It's the guilt I feel for not taking her visions more seriously. It is an impossible task, and I thought if I ignored it, so would Dahlia. If I had seen the pressure she was experiencing, I would have taken active steps with her. We are all still adjusting to the recent changes."

We entered the elevator with several other people and rode to the bottom floor in silence. Being with Noah felt natural as we exited near the emergency room. He led me to the parking structure attached to the building and his truck.

"I'm glad you're giving yourself a break. It's easy to discount things you can't see. What kind of food would you like to eat?" Noah held the door to his truck open and helped me up. At five-foot-three inches, I was short and needed a boost to make it to his seat.

"Honestly, I would love to pick up some fried green tomatoes, fried chicken, and a salad and eat at home. I'm a picky eater and have no desire to be social. It would be nice to take these gloves off and relax." I plucked the end of one fingertip.

Noah grabbed the glove off my hand. I reached for it, but he held it out of the way. "You have been in my car many times and touched just about every surface. You are immune to the space by now. I want you to be yourself here and at my house. I know it is scary for you, but I need you to know all of me. And I want to be a safe harbor for you."

Emotion clogged my throat. I gave up trying to take my glove back and removed the other one, then stuffed it in my purse. "I'm not sure I'm ready for all of that. However, I'm willing to give you some leeway."

Noah leaned over and pressed a kiss to my lips. It quickly deepened as his tongue slid inside my mouth to tangle with mine. I clutched his shoulders without thinking and was glad I wasn't sucked into a vision of him getting dressed. His fingers tangled in my hair and I suddenly wanted to climb into his lap.

He pulled away before I got carried away and sat back. "I'll place an order to pick up. Are you alright going to my place to eat? You've never been there and I want you to see it."

Butterflies took flight in my stomach. His expression told me how important this was to him. There was no reason for me to be so nervous, yet I was. My insides were squirming, and I felt two decades younger. It had been a long time since I felt like this.

Smiling, I nodded my head. "I'd like that. My only promise is to try without the gloves. I cannot promise I will be able to tolerate repeated memories. Especially if they involve you and another woman." I held up my hands as he chuckled and brushed a hand across one of my flaming cheeks. "Don't get me wrong, I'm not a jealous person. I know you have a past, as do I. That doesn't mean I want to witness you getting naked with some woman."

"You never have to worry about that, Sunshine. I have never brought a woman to my place. Females of the pack have come over for one reason or another, but I haven't been intimate with a member of my pack since I was a kid." No way could that be right.

My mouth fell open, and I stared at him as he picked up his phone and typed something into it. How could he say that? No way was I going to believe he hadn't had sex for years. He was too sensual to be celibate.

You've never taken a man to the plantation! I was such an idiot. I shook my head as he pulled out of the parking spot. "I haven't brought anyone to Willowberry, either. How long have you lived in your house? Did you move in recently?"

He shook his head as he drove down the levels of the parking structure. "No, I moved in about six years ago after Lucas took over as alpha."

"How is it possible that you haven't brought a woman home, then? Haven't you been married or mated before?" I was in shock and couldn't recall if he had ever mentioned it to me before.

The look he shot me from the driver's seat was pissed. "I told you I've never been mated. I hadn't found my Fated One before. Watching what Lucas went through with Lilly's mom cured me of the desire to get overly involved with anyone. My home is a sacred place to me. I didn't want someone I was casual about being inside it. You're special, Sunshine."

Warmth flooded me. From anyone else, it would have been some cheesy pick-up line. Noah was being genuine. He truly felt that way about me. Otherwise, he wouldn't have said it.

His words touched me while also making me squirm. I wasn't comfortable with compliments or the touchy-feely stuff. "Finally, someone else sees what I've known my entire life. I only had to wait forty-two years."

Noah threw back his head and laughed. "I'm a selfish bastard because I'm glad no one else has seen the depth of your beauty. Otherwise, we might not have met. Your divorce is what prompted you to find Willowberry, right?"

Talking with Noah was one of my favorite things. "Yep. I'm more bite than bark and went after a dream I'd shared with my sisters for years."

"I'd love to feel your bite." Noah parked on the curb outside a green building and waggled his brows at me.

He was trying to keep the conversation light, which I appreciated. We were discussing heavy topics, which I wanted to do without letting it drag us down, as well. The man was hot and listened to everything I told him. It was a relief that he wasn't bothered by having an honest discussion about a loaded topic without letting it add emotions that didn't need to be there.

"Get me my chicken and I might consider it. I have eaten nothing but pudding all day. Hospital food sucks."

Noah pressed his lips to mine and opened his door. "Wait here. I'll be right back."

I watched as he disappeared into a courtyard. I didn't recognize the building and wondered where he was getting food from. I hoped it was a place owned by supernaturals.

The magical world loved to party and had no qualms about spending money, either. Nedasea was spending a small fortune to throw herself a birthday party. Lucas never balked at the cost of his daughter's wedding and easily added a gazebo because she and Lia wanted one. If we were going to be some kind of amateur detectives, we could also make the Twisted Sisters the official planners for the magical world.

Noah was back within a few minutes, carrying two bags. I opened my door and took them from him. "Thanks, Sunshine," he said and pressed his mouth to mine before going around the car and getting behind the wheel.

The nickname he gave me made me smile. From the day we met, he'd been calling me Sunshine, and I loved it. I was smiling like a loon as he pulled out into traffic, thinking about how it felt like we'd done this a hundred times before. This thing with Noah was in its infancy, and yet everything felt natural with him.

We drove in silence for a few minutes before he turned down a road and pointed out a tan shotgun house with green trim. "Lucas and I are restoring that house right now. It's owned by a witch in your coven, actually."

I scanned the tiny porch and took in the neatly potted plants alongside the three concrete steps leading up from the sidewalk. "The place is gorgeous. I would love to get my hands on something like that and redo the inside. I have found a new love of interior design while overhauling the rooms at Willowberry."

We talked about décor and current trends as he drove outside the city to his house. Thirty minutes later, I had

CADAVER ON CANAL STREET

convinced him to put geometric accents on one of the walls in the living room of the shotgun house.

Noah's house was reminiscent of a Creole cottage. It was painted white with blue shutters rather than the more traditional bright colors. However, it had a covered porch, decorative railing, and two windows that had to belong to a cozy attic bedroom.

I jumped down from the truck before he could help me and grabbed the bags. Taking them from me, he led the way to the front door. A woodsy scent greeted me as we crossed the threshold.

Unlike most Creole cottages, the inside was massive. I could see where he had taken out a wall to create a big open space between the kitchen and living room. The hall was much longer and had more doors than I expected. It was clear he wasn't afraid of color because the inside was a mix of teal and cream. I wondered about the color of the other rooms.

"This place is fantastic. And much bigger than I expected."

Noah shrugged and put the bags on the marble island. "I built onto the original structure. Not that I needed more than three bedrooms. It was something to do with my spare time. Now I have five bedrooms and four full bathrooms."

I pulled the food from the bag and my vision wavered as my hand touched the counter. Noah was standing in front of me, only he was wearing different clothes and Lucas was with him.

"What did you think of the sisters today?" Lucas asked as he sipped a beer.

Noah peeled the label off his bottle. "Dani lit me up like the sun. I've never experienced anything like it. What about you? I saw the way you looked at Dahlia, the one that lives with mine."

"Dani! Come back to me, Sunshine."

I blinked and shook my head as the memory faded. Noah was standing in front of me with my leather gloves hanging from a hand. "Maybe it's too much right now. I haven't even fed you yet. How are we ever going to get to the biting if you stay hungry?"

I flushed at his mention of biting. A smile spread over my face. "I lit you up like the sun, huh?"

Noah's cheeks turned pink, and he lowered his gaze. "Yes. You still do. Eat."

I accepted the plate he handed me while thinking over what I had seen. I only picked up moments tied to intense emotions in people's lives. It was why I saw so much at Willowberry. And it told me that meeting me was big for Noah. That made putting myself out there with him a lot easier. No one wanted to get in too deep and get hurt.

I picked up a piece of chicken and took a bite. Flavor exploded on my tongue and a moan rumbled up my throat. "Mmm. This is delicious. Where did you pick it up, anyway?"

Noah made eating fried chicken sexy. "From the Orange Fox. A witch named Heidi owns it and makes the best fried chicken in town."

My appetite morphed to desire as I watched him lick his lips. "I would agree. This is something else." My next bite was even better as I watched him enjoy the food. He made eating sensual. The man had serious talent.

The tension grew as we ate in silence for several minutes. His eyes undressed me as we sat at the island across from each other. My body reacted, heating and becoming more and more aroused as the seconds passed. Finally full enough that my stomach was no longer growling, I took my plate and rinsed it in the sink. "That was the best fried chicken that I've ever eaten. Aside from my mom's, of course."

Noah finished putting the leftover food in glass containers and set them in the fridge. I was acutely aware of every move he made as he closed the distance between us. I looked up at him, expecting him to kiss me passionately. Instead, he tucked my hair behind one ear and grazed my jawline.

My breathing was choppy, and I was having the mother of all hot flashes. When a fine sheen of sweat covered me from head to toe, he decided to close the remaining space and press his mouth to mine. The kiss was brief before he pulled away and looked at me expectantly.

He was waiting for a cue from me. I was torn. My body screamed at me to take him while my mind said this was far too fast, that I wasn't a young woman without control over her hormones and body.

"I know you have reservations and have been hurt by others in the past. There is so much beyond our control, and how I feel about you is one of them. I can't resist you, Sunshine. You make me burn in ways I never knew possible. You've bewitched me."

I smiled and cupped his cheek. "It's good to hear you say that because I might combust if you don't kiss me again."

It had been a long time since I was overcome by these fluttery feelings. I don't think my heart had ever opened wide. I thought so a few times, but in the end, I knew I was wrong when walking away was easy and relatively painless.

Without letting my mind talk me out of my reaction, I followed my gut and threw my arms around his neck. His arms wound around me and lifted me by my backside. Having my body pressed intimately against his made my desire all the more poignant. I moaned into his mouth as he kissed me.

He was walking down the hall when he broke away from my mouth. My chest heaved as I looked into his green eyes. "We bought Willowberry to start the next adventure in our business and discovered so much more than we ever anticipated. You make me feel things I thought I never would. You set my body on fire in addicting ways."

A sexy smile spread over his face. "In what ways?" He didn't wait for me to answer as his mouth took mine in a rugged, sensual kiss. His lips were insistent and passionate and made me wet faster than a hummingbird flapped its wings.

"Mmmm," I groaned against his mouth.

His hands tightened on my butt cheeks and tugged me against his body. My mouth felt raw as I kissed him from the way his stubble abraded me, and I didn't care. Being with him like this took me back decades and reminded me what new love was like.

Noah moved his mouth and nipped his way to my earlobe. "Do you want me to stop before this gets out of hand?"

My brain was fogged by hormones and need, so my earlier caution was nowhere to be found. "I'll die if you stop now."

His groan had a feral edge and rattled my entire body. "You're making it hard for me to be a gentleman, Sunshine."

No man had ever been more aware of me and how I felt. Deciding to take matters into my own hands, I reached between our bodies and pulled his shirt up over his head. "I'm not professing my undying love to you, just that I want you. Right now."

I tossed his shirt aside, and my gaze became glued to the muscled planes of his chest. Bodies like this existed only in airbrushed magazines. I'd seen him naked before, yet making out with him and on the verge of doing so much more, he was even more gorgeous. My hands went to his skin like a moth to a flame.

"You are perfect," he told me. I flushed and bit my lip to keep from pointing out my imperfections. He would like me for me or not. I wasn't going to fret over them ever again.

Noah grinned and walked forward laying me on the bed. I fought the urge to wiggle as he stood back and watched me. His hands went to my shoes and pulled them off my feet before going for my pants and panties. I lifted my hips, giving him more access while also trying to raise my sweater over my head.

Noah chuckled at my eagerness as he kicked off his shoes and took off his pants. I raised a brow. "Are you leaving those on?" He was still wearing his boxer briefs.

"For now. If I remove them, this will be over faster than I want." Noah laid his body over mine and kissed the side of my neck.

I was alright with moving this along. I was more aroused than I could ever recall. One of my hands went behind my back and unclasped my bra while I tried to push one sock off, using the side of the bed. Something brushed over my clit while I worked, making me gasp.

"Holy crap." I writhed and lifted and moved, trying to get more pressure where I needed it. One sock came off and I managed to get one arm out of my bra.

Noah lifted and his eyes became glued to my bare breast. His groan vibrated through me and his finger increased pressure exactly where I needed it. Abandoning my remaining sock and bra. I pushed the edge of his briefs. They slid down his hips.

I moved my body when I felt the heat of his erection press against the top of my thigh. I wanted that between my legs. He allowed me to move until I felt his cockhead pressed against my opening.

"Protection," I gasped.

Noah paused and replaced it with a finger. "I'm clean and so are you. Paranormals don't carry mundane diseases." That was interestting and worth further follow-up but my mind fractured as he continued. "Need to make sure you're prepared for me." The way his focus shifted more to himself told me that he was lost to the growing passion, as well.

"I've never been more ready in my life."

He chuckled and retook my mouth, his tongue sliding against mine, mimicking how our bodies were joining. The pressure at my core increased, then disappeared. I had no patience for slow at the moment. I wanted him.

I lifted my hips and grabbed his, making him thrust back in, which made him enter me to the hilt in one swift move. I paused for a second, adjusting to his sizable cock. Noah made it easy as he kissed down the side of my neck and went lower.

My hips surged when he licked, then sucked my nipple into his mouth. Just like that, I was on the edge of a mind-blowing orgasm. He pulled out a little, then thrust back inside.

Reassured when he met no resistance, he set a fast and hard rhythm. I wasn't sure whether it was Noah's tongue on my breast or because his cock hit nerves inside me that had never been touched before, but my body coiled tightly in an instant. Damn, he was right. This was going to be over far too quickly.

My heart raced as I chased my climax. I couldn't think beyond the pleasure of the moment, which turned out to be a relief. I tended to get into my head, and I didn't want anything ruining this perfect moment.

It helped that Noah didn't try to make this an emotional encounter. He wasn't making tender love to me, and wasn't spouting touchy-feely promises which was precisely what I didn't need at that moment. I know he sensed that too much would make me shutdown, so he held back while still sharing himself with me. The more tender stuff would come later.

I arched my back, shoving more of my breast into his mouth while moaning loudly. My muscles clamped down on him when I felt one of his fingers reach between our bodies and press over my clit. The man was everywhere at once, hitting every one of my erotic zones at the same time. When he shifted his mouth to my other breast. It was enough to send me careening over the edge.

The orgasm took my breath away. He watched me as my body writhed and I screamed his name. The moment was intense and powerful. A second later, he grunted and jerked above me as his climax exploded from him.

I threw my hands out to the side as I tried to catch my breath. "Does shifter stamina apply to everything?"

Noah laughed as he removed my bra from the other arm and took off the one sock I'd been wearing. "I'm just getting warmed-up, Sunshine." His wicked smile was full of promise.

My heart skipped a beat and my mind threatened to ruin the moment. I wanted to keep things light and easy like they had been. Part of me feared he would turn out to be a jerk like the others. I banished those thoughts and gave myself over to Noah.

CHAPTER 16

*D*ahlia

I hid my reaction to the familiarity with which Noah touched and looked at Dani. One thing my forty-five years of experience had taught me was there was a certain way a guy regarded you after he'd had sex with you. And that was how Noah was with my sister.

My inner romantic was jumping up and down, clapping while the concerned sister in me was holding her breath. I'd watched Dani go through far more than any woman deserved. She was a saint, in my opinion.

She put up with an abusive asshole with her first husband without killing him. It had been touch and go when she left him. The jackass called me and my other sisters daily asking where his wife and children were. Dani hired an attorney, and the rest is a messy history of verbal abuse and him putting the kids in the middle.

I thought she had found a gem in Hugo. He had the patience of Job and never once raised his voice with her. That didn't mean he was a good guy, though. He ignored Dani and constantly pushed her to work more hours so they could pay their bills. We discovered after she left him he had cheated on her. Now I wondered if the affair was his real reason for wanting her to work more than was healthy for a person.

Lucas bent and pressed his lips to mine. "I'm going to pull the car around the front, Flower. The doctor said the nurse will be in soon to discharge you."

I smiled up at him. He hadn't left my side since before I woke up in the hospital. I'd suspected he was a keeper. Now, I knew that to be a fact. "Sounds good. I'm going to have Dani and Cami help me get dressed, so we are ready to go."

"I will be waiting in the pickup area. If it takes longer, text me and let me know."

"Will do," I agreed.

Noah kissed Dani on the cheek, then followed Lucas out the door. Dani's smile vanished the second the door closed, and she rushed to the side of the bed. "Oh my God, Lia. I think I've made a mistake."

I rolled my eyes and clasped her hand. "Take a deep breath. I know you slept with him and I can see how upset you are now. You have done nothing to regret. Noah isn't like other men. You already know this or you would never have gone to bed with him. Give yourself credit for knowing better."

Camilla brought the bag with clothes to the bed and set it down. "Lia is right, Dani. Noah cares for you deeply. Not that I know anything of substance about such things."

Dani pressed her lips together and helped me sit up. "How are you feeling? Any dizziness?"

I rolled my eyes and was relieved there was no pain with the movement. I touched the gauze on my head and noted the tenderness. "Nope. I'm okay."

My heart twisted when those words left my mouth. Our mom had been a rock all throughout the two-plus-year battle with cancer. In the end, when her brain was riddled with tumors, she never complained. Her response, when asked, was always, "I'm okay." The six of us had gotten those words tattooed on our bodies after she passed.

I cleared my throat of the emotion that had lodged there. "I hurt more than I want, but I'm better than I should be. Back to you. Are you truly freaking out about Noah? Because you looked happy and at ease when he was here."

Dani shrugged her shoulders. "I'm worried it's too soon. I know he won't turn into an asshole. However, I promised myself I would remain alone and focus on the business, not another guy."

I was glad to hear Dani hadn't lost the goal she'd set for herself. She needed to know she could succeed and be happy. "I know what you mean. I am not telling you to jump in and mate him. You can have fun and get to know him without him becoming your sole focus in life. We have given up everything for Willowberry, and I'm not about to let you move out and leave me hanging. Now, can you take the IV out so I can use the bathroom? I'd love to shower this muck off."

Dani chuckled and grabbed some supplies from one of the cabinets in the room. "Thanks, sis. I knew I could count on you. Give me your arm."

She was quick about removing the tiny plastic tube from my arm before putting a bandage over the wound. I swung my legs over the edge of the bed and wobbled when I stood up. Dani was right there to steady me.

"Take it easy, Dahlia. We almost lost you three days ago. You aren't fully healed."

I nodded and clenched my jaw. "My ribs are definitely reminding me of that."

Dani stayed close to me and kept her arm around me as we entered the bathroom. I took a seat on the plastic chair in the shower stall and she helped wash my face and body. We were done and drying off when the outer door opened.

Dani stuck her head out while I sat on the toilet and got dressed. "Hey Nancy. Lia's getting dressed, we'll be right out."

"You really should have waited for me, Dani. You don't work here anymore." Nancy had been a great nurse during my stay, so it was surprising to hear her get snippy.

Once I had my clothes on, I shuffled to the door and headed for the bed. Nancy eyed me up and down. "You're moving well on your own, but you are still recovering from a head injury and might suffer dizzy spells, so be careful. Let me go over your discharge instructions."

Camilla put my socks and shoes on while I listened to Nancy tell me how to care for the wounds and when I needed to follow up with Dr. Carrasco. Within minutes, I had a soft beanie over the gauze on my head and was being wheeled out of the hospital.

Lucas was waiting in his truck as he promised. He jumped out and helped me into the passenger side. To my surprise, Noah was in the back, and Cami and Dani joined him.

I sucked in a breath, steeling my nerves as Lucas pulled out of the circular drive. The urgency to find the victim in my vision was relentless. "You guys aren't going to like this, but I am hoping we can go to Canal Street. I don't plan on trying to have a vision. And I'm not hoping to run into the killer of the woman. I was hoping you would use your psychometry to see if either of them frequents the area, Dani."

I was turned with my back to the door and looked at my sister sitting in the middle of the backseat. She grimaced and her shoulders slumped. "This isn't a good idea, Lia. You need to rest and recover."

I reached deep for patience. It helped no one to keep it all in and try to do it on my own. "I know I am in no shape to do much walking. I only want to go to the spot where they were before we head to Kip's place so she can finish healing me."

Dani cocked her head to one side. "Alright. If you promise not to push yourself, I will see if I can learn anything. Tell me who I am looking for because I haven't seen either of them."

I grimaced. Perhaps this wasn't such a good idea, after all. With no other choice, I needed to try. I gave Dani every detail I had about both the woman and the guy. The hospital wasn't far from Canal, and Lucas was pulling into the parking lot we usually used.

"I hope you brought some lube, Luc, because this guy charges thirty bucks to park here regardless of how long we are actually here." I understood parking was expensive down here, but that was a bit much.

Lucas and Noah burst out laughing. Luc was still laughing as he rolled his window down. "Hey, Ricky. Dahlia here has warned me I need lubricant to withstand your prices."

Ricky's smile flashed my way before he focused on Lucas. "I have to pay for my threads somehow, alpha. I didn't know she was yours or I wouldn't have charged her." He looked in the back seat and his green eyes widened. "Who do we have here?"

"This is Dani. She's with me and is Dahlia's sister. And this is Camilla, their friend," Noah gestured to Dani, then Cami.

"It's a pleasure to meet you, Camilla. Feel free to park anywhere, alpha. I'll be sure everyone knows not to charge these women." Ricky was looking at Cami the entire time he was talking.

Lucas rolled his eyes and pulled into a parking spot. "Ricky's a bit of a ladies' man. He isn't the best choice for a

CADAVER ON CANAL STREET

first date after centuries of being dead. I recommend easing into him, Cami."

Cami's eyes widened as she jumped down from the truck and made a squeaking sound. "What do you mean? I'm not dating him."

"No, but the look he gave you expressed his interest," Dani explained. "He wants to get to know you better."

Cami flushed and glanced over at Ricky. "I'm not ready for anything like that. I wouldn't know what to do on a date."

I chuckled and waited for Lucas to help me down from the seat. A shiver wound up my spine as my body rubbed against his when I slid to the ground. I ducked my head and threaded my arm through Dani's. I was in no position to think about the look Lucas had given me just then.

I smiled at Cami, who fell into step next to us. "There's no pressure. We will talk about what dating is like today another time. But be prepared to have many men and women interested in you. You're very pretty."

Cami nodded and watched Ricky as we started down the street. I think she was more interested than she let on, but I agreed that it wasn't the time for her to explore a romantic relationship.

Dani put her free hand over mine. "When did Kip set up the appointment to heal you?"

"She'll be by in the morning." My steps were slow and careful as we walked a few feet down Canal Street. I was out of breath and my ribs were shards of fire in my chest by the time we reached the location I'd seen the dead body.

"Where exactly will the victim be dropped?" Dani asked as she glanced around the area.

I waited for some tourists to pass our group and walked to the wall. "Right here." I scanned the location and noticed a traffic camera. "I think he's familiar with the location, at least because he checked to make sure they couldn't be seen by the camera."

"I don't think he was trying to avoid being taped. We are right in view," Lucas observed. The thought was chilling. That would be a bold move. If that was the case, he wasn't afraid of being caught.

Dani moved around our group and reached out to touch a section of the wall. She gasped and her eyes went vacant. I surged forward but didn't get far when Lucas saved me from falling and Noah caught Dani.

We had to look like loons as we stood around silently watching our friend. Noah gestured with his chin to a café down the street. "Lucas, you and Cami grab some beignets and cocoas, so we look less conspicuous."

Lucas nodded and pressed a kiss to the top of my head. "We will be right back." I was more than happy to let them go. The short walk had done me in. I would need to save my energy to get back to the car.

Dani lifted her hand and sucked in a breath. "Nothing here."

She proceeded to touch the handle on the door to the hotel. I stayed where I was, too sore to move. After a few seconds, she looked at me and shook her head. She repeated the process on a pole, a trashcan, and several of the doors down past the café where Lucas and Cami were exiting with a tray of drinks.

Lucas hurried to my side and handed me a paper cup, then slid an arm around me. "How are you doing?"

"Tired and sore. But that's not why I feel awful. I'm torturing my sister for no reason. She hasn't seen anything, and she looks like she's going to pass out any second. Can you signal Noah to have her stop? I don't want to yell."

Dani's shoulders drooped more and more and dark circles had formed beneath her eyes. She was trying her hardest, despite the toll it was taking on her to help me with this. I knew she wouldn't quit until I told her it was pointless.

Lucas whistled. The sound was low rather than loud and shrill. Noah turned and nodded, then put a hand on Dani's arm. After a brief discussion, they headed back to us.

Dani accepted the drink Lucas offered. "I'm sorry I didn't get anything useful, Lia. I can try later if you want."

I shook my head. "There's no use. You would have seen something if they came here often. I'll be able to come up with a better plan after Kip heals me and I get a good night's sleep. You know how often they wake you when you're in the hospital. I appreciate your help. Especially when it's obvious you're being drained by the process."

"Nothing a beignet can't cure," she replied, and took one of the paper bags from Camilla.

Cami held up the other two bags. Lucas handed Noah a cocoa and tossed the paper carrier in the trash, then took a deep-fried piece of dough from one of the bags and handed it to me. I moaned around a bite as we made our way back to the car.

Dani's phone dinged with an incoming text. She handed her drink to Noah and pulled it from her purse. My heart started racing when a curse left her mouth.

"What is it? Is someone hurt?" My other sisters were fine when they'd visited earlier that day. We hadn't informed our brothers or children about what happened because they didn't know about our magic.

Dani shook her head. "Everyone is fine. It was Kip. She couldn't get through to you and wanted us to know not to come over tonight. Something came up. She said she will stop by the plantation tomorrow with Kaitlyn and heal you."

I nodded and sighed. It was going to be a long night. I hurt all over and wanted some alleviation before it got too bad. I'd refused pain medication in anticipation that I would be all better before my head hit the pillow.

Lucas leaned close to my face. "Don't worry, Flower. I'm not leaving your side. Tell me how I can help you feel better and I will do it."

The prospect of Lucas sharing a bed with me made my entire body flush with heat. I wanted to tell him that wasn't necessary, but couldn't find my words. Honestly, I wanted him there. His presence was comforting, and it would allow Dani to get some sleep.

CHAPTER 17

$\mathcal{D}$anielle

Dreya helped Dahlia to the chair Deandra brought for her from the area between the main house and the big kitchen. "You don't look so good, Lia. Are you sure you should be out here? We could have waited inside for Kip and Kaitlyn to arrive."

We were out in the main yard in front of the house where we would practice spells with Kaitlyn. Dahlia was in no shape to be out here. She was sweating and her pallor was closer to Casper than her usual vibrant color.

Lia sucked in a breath and winced, her free arm wrapped around her chest, right under her breast. "I'd rather be outside. I've been cooped up in a hospital for far too long. It's not much further."

I regretted not having our session in the port cochere where Phi and I built a wall of planters for succulents. We had two vintage, teak, outdoor dining sets placed there to create the perfect spot for the six of us to unwind and relax after a long party. Dre and I had been afraid our errant magic would burn down the house or destroy the tables our grand-father built.

Dre settled Lia into the chair as a car pulled into the parking lot. The front of the main house was behind us and faced a river in the distance, with the parking lot off to the left, behind some trees.

We could see Kip climb out of the blue sedan first, followed by Kaitlyn. It must pay to be the high witch because that BMW had to cost a fortune. Phi chewed on her lower lip. "We should have brought out some drinks and snacks. We aren't being very good hosts."

I winced. She was right. Being raised in the South, our mom drilled proper manners into us from an early age. "Let's go grab the drinks from the fridge in the main kitchen. Dea, can you grab the cheese and meat platter Lucas dropped off earlier for Lia?"

Dea nodded and took off to the house while Phi and I branched off to the big kitchen. We used the fridge there to store drinks and excess food. It didn't take long to reach the kitchen.

I did a double-take when I opened the fridge. "Did you add these bottles of tea?"

Phi shook her head from side to side as she pulled several of the containers from the cooler. "No, I haven't had a chance to go shopping yet. It must have been Lucas and Noah. It is your favorite flavor."

A smile crossed my face as I considered Noah doing this without even telling me. He was thoughtful enough to do something like that. I grabbed a basket and put the tea, soda, and water in it, then we headed back outside.

By the time we reached the group, Dea was back and Dakota had set up a small table with the tray of snacks. I added the basket while watching Kip set up her supplies as she had in the hospital.

Kaitlyn spread a blanket on the ground and gestured to Dahlia. "It will help Kip if you're lying down. Can you manage that?"

Lia nodded and Dre helped her scoot to the blanket and lay down. I knelt next to Dre, and the others followed suit so Dahlia had her five Twisted Sisters along the left side of her body.

Dea was closest to Lia's head and lifted it to remove the soft beanie. "Do you want me to remove the dressings?"

"Yes, please. I will heal the incision and the rest of the bruising. I can't regrow your hair, so you will have a bald spot for a bit," Kip replied without looking up from what she was doing.

Lia lifted a hand and let it fall back down. "It's worth it to be alive right now. Besides, Dani can give me a good cut to make it look intentional."

My stomach roiled. I trained as a hairdresser when I was eighteen, yet hadn't worked in the field in over two decades. I stayed up on techniques and did everyone's hair, but this felt far more important than when I did my oldest daughter's hair on her wedding day. Perhaps it was the reason behind her bald spot that made me so nervous.

I smiled at Lia. "We will figure something out that will keep you beautiful."

Kip took the lid off a jar and smeared a greenish paste over the wound on Dahlia's head, then over the cuts on her arm. Lia lifted her shirt to reveal a gash on her side. Kip covered that, too.

Once that was done, the healer cleaned her hands and held them over Dahlia's stomach. Warm energy flowed from Kip. It was vibrant and earthy. Wildflowers came to mind when I felt her energy.

Dahlia jerked and cried out. The healer remained focused.

"Healing broken bones is a painful process, but it doesn't hurt for long."

Dahlia's jaw was clenched tightly, and sweat covered her brow again. I clasped her hand while Dea brushed the hair from her forehead. We sat like that for a few minutes while the ground beneath us vibrated. Thankfully, Lia's discomfort seemed to ease drastically when the bruising on her face and arms cleared up.

Kip removed her hands and sat back on her heels. "I've done what I could. Your ribs are mended along with the worst of your injuries. You will still have some minor discomfort, but it shouldn't be too bad."

Dahlia sat up and touched the thin pink line on the side of her head. The staples were still there. Phi came running back with a medical kit and handed it to Dea. I hadn't even seen her leave. Dea pulled the staples out and removed the stitches.

Once she was done, Lia reached out and pulled the healer into a hug. "Thank you so much. I can breathe without searing pain."

Kaitlyn clapped her hands. "I hate to be a taskmaster, but I am under a time crunch. Let's practice. And if you get tired or would rather wait, Lia, that's alright. I just want you guys to practice conjuring your witch fire as well as a protection spell. Those two will come in handy, given that you guys tend to attract chaos."

I snorted and helped Dahlia stand up. "That's an understatement. Ever since our magical nature was unleashed, we seem to be magnets for trouble."

Dakota nodded her head. "I'd bet money Marie Laveau is at the center of it. The zombies she sent after us proves she holds a grudge. I'm personally glad I can fry her if she gets close."

Kota spread her fingers, palm up, and light pink flames sparked from the center. I focused on the tingle of energy in my core and imagined flames. Nothing happened. Kaitlyn smiled at Dakota. "Great job. Now put them out."

Kota grunted and the flames were extinguished. "That was much easier this time."

Dahlia cocked her head. "How did you do it? I know Kaitlyn said to connect with the center of our magic, but it seems ambiguous."

"Your witch fire is unique to you," Kaitlyn explained while Kip picked up the blanket and her supplies, then sat down. "Close your eyes and center yourself. Imagine your soul and grab hold of the energy that is brought up when you see it."

I did as she instructed and imagined a bright yellow glow. My fingers tingled when I shifted the image to one of fire. My eyes snapped open, and I shouted, "I did it!" The yellow flames shot into the air, making me catch my breath.

Kaitlyn approached me with a smile on her face. "Good job. Now imagine dousing them with water and putting them out."

I laughed when her advice worked. I watched and Dahlia managed to make amber flames. One by one, my sisters each produced their witch fire. Pride made my chest swell. For a bunch of middle-aged women who had no power a few months ago, we were packing some serious magical mojo now.

"Alright, let's practice a protection spell. Remember, your intent is key to spell casting. Use the chant, *protego,* to block my attack."

I nodded and squared my shoulders, trying to be ready for anything. Dakota shot me a wide-eyed look. I lifted a brow and shrugged my shoulders. I trusted she wouldn't injure us and if she did, the coven healer was there.

Kaitlyn spat something under her breath and I shouted the spell in reaction. Little lightning bolts hit an invisible barrier around Phi, who was next to me while they struck me in the upper shoulder.

"Crap," I exclaimed as I rubbed the sting.

Kaitlyn continued and Dre yelped, followed by Dahlia. I danced out of the way when the bolts came my way. I was breathing heavily and my side hurt from the exertion, but I never could block the attack.

Kip sat back sipping iced tea while eating cheese and crackers and watching us. I wanted to drag a chair over and join her. Magical practice wasn't for the weak or out of shape.

"Let's put that one aside for now. The next spell is far more difficult. Many witches cannot manage this spell, but I have a feeling that at least one of you will be able to do this one. It doesn't have a chant associated with it. You need to focus on your astral body and projecting it outside of yourself."

I lifted an eyebrow, certain it would be too advanced for any of us. I followed Kaitlyn's directions and sat down, then pictured the yellow of my soul and pushed it outside of my physical body.

I tried several times, then cracked an eyelid and watched my sisters. I expected Deandra to be the first to do this one, given her ability to see spirits others couldn't. I was wrong about that.

Delphine suddenly slumped to the side and Dea cried out. I crawled toward Phi along with Dre and felt around her head and chest. "What happened?"

Dea lifted a finger and pointed. "She's there. Phi astral projected."

My head swiveled in the direction Dea was pointing, but I saw nothing. "Why can't we see her?"

Kaitlyn smiled and held her hand up. "It takes significant energy and practice to make yourself visible in your astral form. Good work, Phi. No, rejoin your body. All you need to do is picture what it feels like to be inside your skin."

A second later, Delphine gasped and sat up. "That was freaking cool. I could see you guys and hear everything."

I redoubled my efforts and managed to block the lightning as we continued to practice for another few hours. After Kip and Kaitlyn left, I turned to my sisters. "Can you guys stay for dinner and midnight margaritas? I could use one."

Dakota sat in one of the teak chairs near the succulent wall. "I'm in. Jeff is traveling for work until Friday, so it's just me."

Delphine and Deandra agreed to stay as well. We made a quick dinner of tacos and brought the food and drinks out to the teak tables. Dahlia dashed back inside before we got started and came back with the bags of sweatshirts that we had made for everyone.

"What's this?" Dreya asked as she pulled out the grey top with a design in black vinyl that said *Midnight Margaritas* with a bottle of tequila, a mortar and pestle and several stars and moons. Another aspect I loved about the laser was that we could cut designs out of heat transfer vinyl and press them onto any article of clothing we wanted.

Lia inclined her head to me and gave me her go-ahead look. "Dahlia and I made these the other day. We thought they were perfect for nights like this."

We had been nicknamed the Twisted Sisters because of our sense of humor, as well as our desire to have matching shirts. Everywhere we went, one of us made tops for everyone. One of my favorites was the ones Phi made, describing our role in the family. I was the crafty one.

Dakota squealed and pulled it over her head. "These are

fantastic. You know my girls are going to want one now, right?"

Lia chuckled. "I figured. I ordered their sweatshirts already. I just have to make them."

"Too bad Kaitlyn didn't teach us a spell to cut out the vinyl. That's the longest part of the process and as many things as we make with it, we could use it."

Deandra had a point. We were constantly creating things with heat transfer vinyl. Lia even created interchangeable shapes for a tall welcome sign for porches. We used to paint the trees, hearts, and eggs, but she applied the vinyl and it transformed them.

Dreya scoffed. "We'd have ended up covered in the stuff if we had tried."

I laughed at that. "We have power and little control. Mom always said practice makes perfect. I'm almost afraid to keep at it with the spells. Losing control of the flames like Kota did that first time is a terrifying thought."

Dahlia tilted her head to the side. "That's the problem. We need to set aside our mundie notions and fear. It's impeding us."

Delphine stuffed a guac-covered chip into her mouth and nodded to the back of the property where the rundown buildings were located. "You make a good point. But should we stay clear of the new pixie mound when we practice? We have little control and it would suck to blow up their new home."

Deandra burst out laughing. "That's a very likely outcome. Did you see Dani with her sunny flames? She almost burned her hair off."

Dahlia started laughing, and the others joined her. I followed suit because her laughter was contagious. We sat eating tacos and giving each other shit about our burgeoning magical abilities.

It was the perfect ending to an eventful day. We had all managed to perform magic during our practice with Kaitlyn. Our flames combined, closely matched the colors of a rainbow. We were not only family, but the Six Twisted Sisters were also undoubtedly a mystically connected group, and I was proud to be one of them.

CHAPTER 18

Dahlia

My body might be healed, but I still had no energy. The problem was, we didn't have time for me to lie around resting. We had a big party to get ready for and a new client to meet with.

I took another layer of the conch shell off the laser engraver and set it on our work table for Dani to spray paint. Nedasea had decided on teals, sea-greens, and blues for most of the signs, with the table cloths being an iridescent white.

"We need to order the flowers before this Friday, so we are certain they have the ones we need." Dani was shaking the can of dark teal and checking the layers already on the drying rack.

I put the next piece of plywood into the machine. "I agree. I think we have enough seahorses, starfish, and angelfish. Do you think we should do others?"

The door to the silo opened, and the siren bounded into the space followed by Dreya. What the hell was going on? We generally didn't allow clients in our workspace. I hit start on the laser and walked toward them.

Dani stopped spraying the shell and joined us. Dreya lifted a hand and pointed to the bags in Nedasea's hands. "Neda brought some glasses she wants us to engrave for the party."

I took a deep breath. She had previously agreed to use some rocks glasses we had. I'd spent ten hours engraving them last night with various nautical images and the words bon voyage.

Dani lifted a brow. "Okay. We just finished the other glasses there, as you can see." She pointed out the hundred glasses on a few of the shelves we used for party prep.

Neda set the bags down and picked up one of them. "I love them. They're perfect. And, I still want to use them. But I found some blue ones with a seahorse as the stem and couldn't resist. There's only twenty-five of these, so not enough for everyone to have one."

The siren set the glass on the shelf and pulled a paper-wrapped bundle from her bag and handed it to Dani, who unwrapped the item. "This is gorgeous. And perfect for the party. I can see why you wanted to buy these."

I ran a finger over the seahorse and nodded. "What would you like engraved on these? More of the same?"

Neda tilted her head to the side and pursed her lips. She was quiet for so long, I didn't think she was going to say anything. Dani shot me and Dre a questioning look. Before either of us could so much as blink, the siren broke her silence.

"I don't want the same thing on these. The first batch is a farewell to my previous life. These hold a piece of my past, but make me think of my future and I have no idea what I would like to put on them."

Dani held up the blue glass. "We could put seize the day, only use SEAS instead. It tells people to look forward and go after their goals."

Nedasea's face lit up. "I love it. Let's go with that."

I grabbed the plywood I'd engraved with about fifty font samples. I discovered long ago that people have a hard time selecting the right one, but if I give them no choice, they often come back with complaints.

Holding up the board, I pointed to the middle. "Which font do you want that in? And what do you think about adding a conch shell to these? We didn't put any on the others, so these would be unique."

The siren scanned the samples. "Oh my, this is hard. It was easier when you showed me the three choices last time. There are too many choices here."

I chuckled. "This isn't even half of them. There are literally thousands. I am thinking we use a combination of cursive and print to emphasize Seas."

The siren smiled and clapped her hands. "Perfect. Use this font for Seas and I don't care which print you use. Do you have business cards I can hand out to friends? I've already had numerous people ask about you guys."

Dani had a stack in her hand and hesitated to hand them over. I loved the image of a twister with flowers, champagne glasses, and ribbon at various points. "We should get some new ones made. Ones that we hand out to paranormal clients only. These seem plain and boring compared to what magical people would expect."

I laughed at Dani's furrowed brow. "It's not like magic can make a business card glow or talk."

The siren shrugged her shoulders. "Actually, as witches, you should be able to make them do both. Although talking isn't really necessary. I've seen many with messages that are only revealed to paranormals. Most often, it's an address that remains hidden from mundies, so our world isn't accidentally revealed."

"I never thought about how that might work. Is there a

paranormal only Facebook or something?" It stood to reason that they had everything we did. For some reason, I never stopped to consider there was an infrastructure to the magical world.

Without change, there was no life. I didn't like embracing change and rolling with it, but I was damn good at it after the life I'd had. Having a husband murdered made me realize every moment mattered and sweating anything made me miss out on way too much.

Neda nodded her head. "We use the same Facebook like everyone else, but there are several private groups that you will want to join. There's one for just about every major city. It's the easiest way to stay up to speed on shit."

Dre shook her head with a chuckle. "And here I was thinking you all had some kind of telepathic way of communicating."

The siren narrowed her eyes. "I can't tell if you're joking or not."

Dreya smiled. "I was poking fun. However, I guess I anticipated some magical way of disseminating information. When you can move objects with your mind or ensnare someone with a song, it seems like it should be possible."

Nedasea scowled and crossed her arms over her chest. "I haven't used my song to take someone's life energy for decades. Refraining is a point of pride for me. And the reason this celebration is so important."

Dre held up her hands with wide, pleading eyes. "I meant nothing by it. I've heard you are one of the strongest paranormals in the city to be able to live as you do. I admire that. I only wanted to point out that I've seen the impossible become possible, so I never pictured limits on the magical world."

Nedasea dropped her arms as a smile spread across her

face. "I've never considered it from that point of view. It's wild to consider life from a mundie perspective."

"It's a major learning curve. The situation with the vampires at Final Swallow could have turned out badly for us," Dani added. "We owe you for coming to our rescue. We will be better prepared in the future."

The siren clapped Dani on the shoulder. "You guys did great resisting their thrall. Your strength is another thing the community is talking about. It's drawing as many people as your parties. However, you'll want to create a group for paranormals only. Shit will happen that you can't put on your regular pages."

My mind whirled with a dozen questions, but I held back from asking the siren. I'd ask Kaitlyn. She was our head witch and wouldn't judge us for how much we needed to know. "We are working on that so we can share bits and pieces of your birthday bash. We are set for food and dessert. Are you still alright with Brezok being the bartender?"

"I give Brezok a hard time, but he really will be the perfect person to have an arrangement with for events like this. He needs new adoration to survive and your parties will give that to him. He had to offer. If I asked him, then I would owe him a favor and you never want to owe a demon. Not even a fame demon. You never know what they'll ask for in return."

Nedasea's words made me shiver. Dreya chewed on a thumbnail while giving me a what-the-hell look. "Sounds like he isn't the best idea to add to our list of contractors. The last thing we need is for him to weasel favors out of our clients. We won't be a party to anything of that nature."

Neda sucked in a breath. "I didn't explain that very well. Brezok would never try to manipulate your customers like that. He wouldn't risk losing your arrangement. By working for you, you will introduce him to paranormals he never would meet otherwise. You know, only a certain type of person hangs out in a seedy bar. But if he is asked for favors, he always asks for one back. It's like in demon DNA or something."

I lifted the lid on the laser when it beeped and picked up the next layer. "That makes sense. If we gave everyone we knew free parties, we would never have been able to make a business out of what we love doing."

Dani nodded in agreement. "We will have him sign a contract saying he won't get into conversations about favors with anyone while working for us."

Neda shrugged her shoulders. "That'll work. He's an honorable fame demon. Besides, Brezok will be too busy putting on a show for your customers to worry about much else. When he isn't pressured by a busy club, he's very entertaining."

He'd have to be if he survives on fame. I still couldn't truly understand what that meant. Perhaps one day I would ask him. There were far more important things to learn first.

I thought of Lucas insisting we had shifter protection and wanted to test the waters about customer reactions. "We've been interviewing for bouncers and are considering hiring some shifters. Would you have a problem with that?"

Nedasea shook her head from side to side. "No problem at all. Shifters make great protectors. They're powerful and have built-in weapons. You're smart to consider safety. You never know what can happen when a bunch of paranormals get together to party. Better to be safe than sorry. Your customers will appreciate it, too. We all know how shit can take a wrong turn in a second."

Dani held out a few of our cards. "If there's nothing else, we need to get back to preparations for your party. We want this to be perfect. For now, share these cards. We will look into getting new ones soon."

Neda accepted them, then left. We followed her to the

port cochere and showed her where we were going to set up, then watched her leave. Dani removed her cell from her back pocket. "I'm going to ask Kaitlyn about getting some enchanted cards. It would be badass if the twister rotated and different party images surfaced as it circled."

And so it began. One idea from Dani, and the inspiration started flowing. She kick-started the creative side of me. It did the same for the others, as well. Dreya threw out a couple of thoughts, then I added mine.

My fatigue didn't vanish, but it receded to the background as we fed off each other, thinking of the best images and colors for the cards. I thrived when I worked with my sisters. I was capable of far more than I ever knew. And I tried things I never would have without them.

It was the excitement they sparked in me, combined with the knowledge that they believed in me and valued me. It freed me to be myself and share my thoughts without fear of being judged. It was one of the reasons they were the best gift my mother ever gave me.

CHAPTER 19

*D*ahlia

"I can't explain why, but something inside me is screaming that this woman is going to be killed soon." I tried to temper my tone, but didn't succeed.

It was that Dani was asking for the hundredth time for clarification that made me snippy. It was the urgency riding me. It was like another voice in my head. One that had a bullhorn and the compassion of an Olympic coach pushing a swimmer to try harder.

I was very familiar with those coaches and demeanors like that since my youngest daughter recently made her nationals cut for her two-hundred-breaststroke. The next stop was the Olympic trials for her. I might have taken her twice daily to practice for decades, but it was her coaches that were pushing her to excel.

Dani sighed and squeezed my hand as we turned down another street in the French Quarter. We were below the business district and in more of the residential area, searching for the street I'd seen in my vision.

"I know that Kip healed you, but the bags under your eyes tell me you're on the verge of collapse. I just think there is a point where we need to call it quits and return home."

I scanned the people around us for anyone that looked familiar and shrugged my shoulders. "You're right, I am exhausted. However, I'm not giving up yet. She will die if I do."

Lucas's hands landed on my shoulders from behind and rubbed them. "Okay, let's talk this through. It's unlikely he's going to kill her in the open like this. If you saw her in this area, perhaps he lives around here. Or she does."

Noah twined his fingers with Dani's and stepped into the street to walk along her other side. "And if I were a killer, I'd do it in the privacy of my home. Or in a location, I was relatively certain I wouldn't be discovered. Should we start knocking on doors?"

I snorted and shook my head. "That'll take forever. There is no way to go door to door, but I like the idea of it happening in a more remote location. I was hoping to come across her and warn her about Blade. So, where else should we check? It can't be too far from the area. I don't see him driving long to dump her body."

"I'd still like to know *why* he drops her on a busy street to be discovered like that," Dani added. "Most murderers don't want to be caught. It doesn't seem like a crime of passion given that choice."

A chilling thought crosses my mind. "You don't think it's a serial killer, do you?"

Dani's eyes widened. "Are there paranormal serial killers? You said he had to be a shifter, given the claw marks across her chest."

Lucas's hands warmed me as they continued to knead the tense muscles. "Life is different in the magical world, and many have taken a life. We consider the zombies you and your sisters killed the other night lives you've taken, but I wouldn't call you mass murderers because of the number of beings you took out. It's an interesting question. What makes one a serial killer?"

Noah cocked his head to the side. "I would consider any being that kills for joy and not to survive or defend themselves a serial murderer. Even in our world, we can draw the line at doing it for the excitement. It's what makes demons so dangerous and hated."

Lucas removed his hands, and I almost begged him to continue the massage. "Good point. That being said, what about searching the parks for this guy? Most are deserted at night and would be good places to kill someone."

I felt better having a new direction to search. "Let's check the one at the end of Canal first. The acres of green space, not the businesses." Given he would dump her on that street it seemed like a good start, even if it was unlikely given how close it was to the hustle and bustle of the Quarter.

Dani nodded in agreement. "I was going to suggest that one, too. There aren't as many trees to offer cover, but paranormals are capable of hiding right in front of our eyes. And, it's close."

Lucas shrugged his shoulders and turned us in the direction of the park, which just so happened to be close to where we parked the car. The guys were on a mission, and it was a struggle for Dani and me to keep up with their long strides.

Lucas slowed before I could ask. "Sorry, Flower. I didn't realize how fast we were walking. Do you need to take a break?"

"No, but a piggyback ride would be nice." My chest was heaving as I sucked in oxygen and I was covered in sweat. "Kidding. Let's just slow it a fraction." I had no desire for him to experience the swamp thing just yet. He had to be head over heels for me before that happened.

We walked through Woldenberg Park and discovered a couple making out, and a few pixies but not much else. Thankfully, we were parked close by and got in the car to check the other locations.

My heart sank further and further as we checked each one. I had high hopes for Louis Armstrong Park, but it, too, gave us nothing. I sat in the backseat thinking about what would be good locations for someone to kill a young woman.

The thoughts were morbid, but my sisters and I had watched enough of what we called *murder, death, kill* shows to have a rudimentary understanding of the criminal mind. That, combined with my study of serial killers in college, had my mind churning.

"Let's try Loyola and Tulane. I know it's likely too cliché for a paranormal murderer, but a college campus has historically been a popular spot to kill a young coed and the victim fits that bill," I suggested.

Dani sucked in a breath. "We should have thought of that sooner. Most college students are still downtown partying at this hour, so campuses are empty. It was always eerie when I studied late in the library."

The drive through Loyola came up empty and as we turned into one of the parking lots for Tulane, I was about to give up and go home when I spotted the car from my vision across the large lot.

I lifted a finger and pointed to the vehicle. "He's here! Look, that's his car. I can't believe he's hunting on a college campus and killing mundies."

Noah shook his head from side to side. "Paranormals attend here as well. How do you think they get trained for various jobs? Witches aren't capable of giving us skills and a history needed to run a business or perform surgery so we study the same as mundies."

Lucas parked his truck close to the guy's car. "They do, however, sell glamours so a fame demon or elf can mask the oddities that would oust them as other."

I looked at my sister. "No, we aren't adding a backroom to the gift shop for potions and charms. We have enough different avenues to manage."

Dani threw her hands up and gave me her what-are-you-talking-to-me-for look. "I would never suggest something we have no ability to create. I can't promise anything once we learn potions and charm making, though."

I rolled my eyes and threaded my arm through hers as we headed toward the campus. There were green spaces with grass and trees interspersed throughout the campus. We took the path near the Richardson Building and paused before we walked out onto the Gibson Quad.

I went to school here, so I was familiar with the layout. The quad was the largest green space on campus, so I doubted they'd be there. "Can you hear anyone nearby?" I pressed my mouth to Lucas's ear to avoid alerting anyone else of our presence.

He shook his head at the same time his nostrils flared. "I smell something off."

"There's a witch somewhere close, too," Noah interjected in a low voice.

We walked out into the green area, sticking close to the Richardson Memorial. I scanned the night but didn't see much. Not all of my senses were heightened when my dormant genes were activated.

When Lucas and Noah picked up their pace, I looked at Dani and we hurried to catch up. They were heading toward Gibson Hall, which was the oldest building on campus. Was there a paranormal connection to the building?

That thought escaped my mind as the guys started running. Dani was pumping her arms and moving as slow as I was. "Did you hear anything?"

I was out of breath and unable to respond, so I shook my head. We were making more noise than a herd of elephants and I winced, knowing we had to have given our location away.

I watched Lucas and Noah continue around the building. They had to be headed to the greens in front of Gibson that faced St. Charles Avenue. That was more out in the open than I would have expected.

I heard the screams as we reached the sidewalk leading around the side of the building. My lungs burned like the pits of hell, and my side hurt as bad as when I had broken my ribs, but I couldn't stop.

Dani was sucking wind next to me and grabbed my arm when I stumbled and almost fell. That first step off the sidewalk was a doozy. We crossed the u-shaped drive, happy to see the few parking spots there empty.

My feet stopped moving when we reached the edge of the grass. In the middle of the area, Noah was fighting with the big guy I'd seen in my vision while Lucas was bent over the woman who was lying on the ground.

My heart was racing from the run and now the adrenalin that dumped into my bloodstream. We found the woman and her killer. Were we too late? My stomach roiled as I considered the question. I can't have come this far to fail her now.

Dani tugged me into motion again, and we started running to Lucas. Before we reached him, I heard a snarl as Noah shifted into his wolf. Clothes exploded around him as skin became fur and hands became claw-tipped paws. The guy shifted into a wolf a second later. It was impossible to tell the two apart.

Both were black and white and had the same green eyes.

One of them let out a howl as blood flew from his flank. That got Lucas's attention. His head snapped up and his grey wolf took over a second later.

Dani and I reached the woman as Lucas lunged for the fighting wolves. The growls made me cringe while the sight of the woman with gashes across her torso made the bile rise in the back of my throat.

"They aren't as deep as in my vision. She might be alive." I prayed that was the case. I couldn't be too late. "I knew I should have been looking more. Dammit."

Dani knelt next to the woman and pressed one hand over her wounds while she checked her pulse. "She's alive, and that's thanks to you. We need to act fast to save her. Her pulse is thready. Come, put pressure on her wound so she doesn't bleed out while I call Kaitlyn and check her over."

I dropped to my knees next to them and put both hands on her torso when Dani lifted hers. I listened as she called Kaitlyn and gave her a rundown of the situation then asked for Kip's address.

A loud screech drew my eye to the fight a few feet away from us. One of the black and white wolves shifted into a gold and black dragon and swiped a massive talon at Lucas. He leaped out of the way and the injured wolf, who I now knew was Noah, clamped his jaws around the back of the dragon-wolf shifter's ankle.

Purple blood dribbled out of the puncture wounds on the dragon's foot. The killer kicked and Noah went flying. He yelped as he hit a tree. I remained in place while Dani ran to Noah as he landed on all fours.

The dragon blew fire at us, then took off over the campus. I threw my hands over my head, certain we were going to burn to death. The flames singed my hands before going out. It was then that I recalled the protection spell

Kaitlyn had taught us. I should have used it. Resorting to magic wasn't my first thought.

My palms stung as I pressed them over the woman's wounds. "Are you alright, Lucas? We need to get her to Kip. Dani got the address. Can you go get the truck?"

Lucas's wolf ran his muzzle along my arm before he took off in the direction of the car. A naked Noah limped toward me, with Dani helping hold him upright. "Is she alive?"

I kept my gaze focused on the woman. I had no desire to see more of Dani's boyfriend than I already had. "Yes. The injuries are bad but haven't killed her yet. Lucas is getting the truck. How are you?"

Noah grunted. "I'll heal in no time. I'm sorry for doubting you, Lia. You have one powerful ability guiding you. I didn't believe it when your sisters said your smell-o-vision was making you become some kind of paranormal detective, but now I know they were right."

Dani groaned. "That's right. My sister's a badass. I'm going to need to start running again. I can't afford to be that far behind next time."

I nodded in agreement. "Me too. But every one of us Six Twisted Sisters are spark plugs of power and, like the party business, we each have a role to play to make this work."

Lucas pulled into the round between the green and the building. I let Noah pick the woman up. We jumped in the car. I took the back with the injured woman, and Dani, who immediately pressed her hands to the wounds. "Let's not set out a Private Detective shingle anytime soon, m'kay?"

I shook my head and brushed the matted blonde hair from the woman's face. "We can't do that. There's no way to support ourselves with cases like this. I'm not gonna charge this woman after saving her life. We will only handle what is directed our way via my smell-o-vision."

Noah turned in the front passenger seat. I could see a t-shirt on his bicep, so I assumed he'd gotten dressed. "You might get cases from your psychometry, as well. I wouldn't rule that out, either."

Dani furrowed her brow. "Why would we do that? I see the past, not the future."

Noah shrugged his shoulders. "Just because it's the past doesn't mean it's something you should ignore. You might see something you need to fix."

Dani inclined her head. "You might be right, but that's a concern for another day. Right now, we need to save this woman." Dani gave Lucas the address and he took off down the street.

We pulled up in front of a dark blue house with a purple door. My door was open, and I was on the sidewalk before Lucas could join me. He took the woman from Dani and headed to the front door.

My stomach roiled when I went to smooth my top and noticed my hands were covered in blood. Kip opened the door before we even reached it. "Oh, my gods. Stacia! Get her inside."

The frantic way the healer said her name broke my heart and told me she knew her. It made me even more grateful I listened to the voice nagging me to do something about the murder.

We walked inside, and I took in the place. The house's interior had an open plan, with the living room and kitchen sharing one ample space. The smell of herbs filled the air. I looked at the stove and saw a black pot simmering on one of the burners. I wondered what she was making.

Kip crossed to the kitchen counter where dozens of bottles sat along with first aid equipment. Kip pointed to the kitchen table that had been cleared and had a black cloth covering it. "Set her here. What attacked her? I do not recognize the energy."

"It was a wolf-dragon shifter," I blurted.

She scowled at me while Lucas shook his head. "There is no such thing as a wolf-dragon shifter."

The door opened and Kaitlyn ran inside, then gasped when she caught sight of who was on the table. "It was Stacia who was going to die? Holy shit. The killer has to be back."

Dani and I shared a glance. "What killer? Why didn't you mention this when I told you about my vision?"

Kaitlyn placed a hand over Stacia's. "It's been over a year since Stephanie was killed. I assumed it was a one-off despite the nagging feeling telling me it was more than that."

Kip placed her hand over the wounds. Warm energy flowed from her. The same earthy feel crawled across my senses that I experienced when she healed me. The healer lifted her gaze to Kaitlyn. "It was a skinwalker."

Kaitlyn's face lost all color. "No, it can't be. They're legends."

Lucas's expression was grave when he looked at the head witch. "There's no other explanation. The guy shifted into Noah's wolf before it changed into a gold and black dragon. It isn't possible for a couple to have a child capable of shifting into both entities. One set of genes always dominates another."

"Shit," Kaitlyn cursed as she ran her hand down her face. "We could be screwed."

My hands shook as I clenched them into fists. "Someone needs to explain this to us. What is a skinwalker, and why are we screwed?"

Lucas took one of my hands. "They're demonic beings that can shift into anyone or anything once they get a sample of their DNA. They can appear as a man or woman, cat or dog. Or even an alligator. They thrive on magical energy and can only survive in areas with a dense magical population like our fair city."

"And they usually leave a bevy of bodies in their wake," Kaitlyn shared unhelpfully. "My grams told me a story she heard as a child that a skinwalker destroyed an entire city. They're bad news and if we have one here, we're in big trouble."

I breathed a sigh of relief as I saw the skin on Stacia's torso knit together. I'd done it. I saved her life. "Is this the type of situation Phoebe would be called in to handle?"

Kaitlyn moved to Stacia's head as the woman started moaning. "The Pleiades witches are the only ones capable of dealing with a skinwalker."

Dani shook next to me. "Is it possible it's something else?"

Kip, Kaitlyn, Noah, and Lucas all shook their heads. Stacia chose that moment to open her eyes. "Kaitlyn? What happened? Where are we?" Her gaze landed on me and Dani and her brow furrowed.

Kaitlyn patted the woman's shoulder. "You're safe. You were attacked on campus. Do you remember that?"

Stacia sucked in a breath. "I remember this guy Blade from one of my classes talking to me outside the Gibson building and then waking up here. Someone attacked me?"

"It was Blade," I told her, recalling the name from the vision. It was surreal to be talking to her after seeing her dead body every time I closed my eyes.

Kaitlyn gestured to me. "Dahlia had a vision of your murder and managed to find you and save you in time."

Stacia's eyes widened. "He never did feel quite right to me. I should have followed my gut. Thank the gods for leading you to me. I owe you my life."

I waved her words away. "I'm just sorry we didn't find you sooner. And I'm beyond happy that you didn't end up as the cadaver I saw on Canal Street."

Kaitlyn asked Stacia a few more questions and my eyes began to droop. Now that she was safe, the fatigue caught up with me. We said our goodbyes with a promise to talk soon and involve Phoebe and Aidoneus.

I sagged against Lucas as we left the house. Before my eyes slipped closed, I said a silent prayer that the skinwalker had left New Orleans entirely after we intervened. If not, I hoped Phoebe's boyfriend, Aidoneus would be able to locate the son of a bitch.

CHAPTER 20

*D*anielle
My attention wandered from decorating to Dahlia. She'd been back to her old self after we had stopped the skinwalker from killing the woman from her visions. As much as I fought it, I had accepted our lives involved more than just the party planning arm of the Six Twisted Sisters.

It felt good to save a woman from being killed. And in the process, we had uncovered a very serious danger to the city. I knew we hadn't seen the last of it. I was just glad it wasn't something we would have to deal with alone. We weren't equipped to battle a powerful demon.

The ladder wobbled beneath my hands as Deandra stretched on her tiptoes to pin the balloon arch in place over the teal backdrop. The pearl and foil balloons finished the setting perfectly. It was the first time we had created such a thorough under the sea themed event, and my favorite feature was the backdrop with its various fish and bubbles secured to the fabric with magnets.

Dea leaned back slightly and shook her head. "Is that straight?"

I let go of the ladder I was steadying and stepped back. "It's perfect, as always. You attached that one in less than five minutes."

Dea laughed and climbed down. "The entire process is much faster here. where we don't have to move things around to make your visions work."

The hardest part of the process for me used to be adjusting the plan I developed in my mind to fit the space we were working with at the time. I never knew precisely what we had to work with and what we would need until the day of the party, so I always overbought and planned more than necessary. I refused to have a section left without décor when we were done.

"We saved twenty-five percent more than we typically spend on a party like this and we have more going on," Phi pointed out as she adjusted the blue seahorse glasses on the wooden a-frame we used to display drinkware for events.

Dahlia and Dreya adjusted the giant conch shell that served as another backdrop for pictures. It was surrounded by coral and had Nedasea's name in the center of the shell. Neda would take the shell home as our gift to her. The rest of the laser-cut signs we had made would be added to the barn and stored for future use.

Having an entire structure to organize and store our stock made it much easier to reuse the stuff we had already made. Phi was right about saving money. Most of the fish and bubbles came from previous parties. We just painted the wooden shapes colors to match the scheme for this party.

Dakota shifted the hurricane centerpieces next to the flowers. "Clean-up will be easy, as well. Holy shit. You guys weren't kidding. He really does look like a devil."

I followed Kota's gaze and saw Brezok unloading a massive set of shelves from the back of his truck. "How did he drive here without being noticed?"

Lia shrugged her shoulders. "Probably one of those glamour charms Noah mentioned."

Brezok looked up and waved our way. "You are correct, Dahlia. Should I wear my charm while here?"

"So many of the myths about supernaturals are true," Phi pointed out. "The glamour will not be necessary unless we ask you to cover a mundie party. The shelving is a good idea. It'll keep the area around the bar better organized."

Years ago, we had Phi's husband, Tucker, build a teak structure with shelves beneath the top. It was rarely enough space, but it had been easy to transport and hid the mess from guests.

"He's not evil, right?" Deandra whispered next to me.

I arched a brow and waited to see if he heard her. When he said nothing, I shook my head and leaned closer to her. "He feeds off attention."

"He must be getting a feast right now," Dreya replied.

Brezok set the shelving unit down and bowed to me. "Indeed, I am. I assume I should set up behind that bar there?"

Dre nodded her head. "Yes, unless you need us to move you somewhere else."

He scanned the area and noted where Nedasea was helping the band set up close to the fountain. She wanted her dance floor to be near the water. There was plenty of space and it was a good distance from the food, so people could have conversations while they ate without having to shout.

We already had the food tables set up right outside the kitchen and chafing dishes on the warmers. Everything was done except Brezok and the alcohol. The fame demon said something to Dreya, but I was distracted by a slew of headlights turning into the parking lot.

The guests were arriving. Phi and Lia headed to the kitchen where they would make sure the food and dessert platters remained full. Dakota and I went to let Nedasea know her guests were arriving while Dre and Dea went to man the gift table.

Nedasea beamed at us as we reached her. "This is perfect! You guys gave me exactly what I wanted. It is everything I dreamed of, and more for this day."

The siren was a vision in her short silk dress that clung to her curves and matched the green in her hazel eyes. She had long, shiny hair that every woman wished she possessed.

"It's good to know we haven't lost it with all the chaos that has descended upon our lives," I replied with a smile. "Your guests are arriving if you would like to greet them. Dea and Dre are at the gift table and will move them inside once everyone arrives, so they aren't left unattended while you celebrate. If you need anything during your event, we will be near the kitchen ensuring the food stays warm and available."

Neda tugged me into a hug, then did the same to Kota and raced off as the first people arrived. Kota and I stood there as the DJ started playing a popular song. Unlike what we were used to, the volume was moderate and didn't vibrate the souls of my black boots as I stood close to the speakers.

That was not typical for a mundie event. Usually, the music was loud enough to rattle the fillings in my back teeth. "This is nice. I could get used to hosting for paranormals."

Kota pursed her lips. "I'd agree. The wedding was the easiest event we've ever thrown. And this one was a breeze, too. It seems as if they're easier to deal with than mundies."

We'd picked up on the lingo quickly for several reasons. First, to fit in better with the magical world. But also, because it helped us understand what they were saying to us. Something stuck, regardless of how new they were to us.

The DJ leaned forward, and I noticed wings fluttering behind his back. "That's because we haven't ever had an organized place with options like this. Before you get busy,

I'd like to have you guys throw a baby shower for my sister next month. Here's my card."

I took the paper rectangle. "You're an accountant, Drake?"

He inclined his head. "I am indeed. Do you need someone to help with your taxes?"

I looked at Dakota, then back at him. "Yes, actually, we do. This is the first year owning Willowberry and Dahlia will be too busy to try and do our taxes. Besides, I have a feeling it's more complicated now."

Drake laughed, and his amber eyes sparkled. "I'd be happy to help. Perhaps I can get a discount on the party."

Dakota cocked her head to the side. "Do you hide your wings and eyes using glamour, too?"

He nodded his head, and his grin widened. "Those of us that work in the mundie sector use amulets. I use one when I meet with clients, but I work from home most of the time. Looks like things are getting underway. I'm going to grab some food before it's gone."

We thanked him and followed after him at a slower pace. I scanned the party-goers and Nedasea, noting how she glowed brightly as she laughed and talked to her friends. Dre and Dea were carrying the gift table inside the back door to keep the presents safe and out of the way.

A couple of guys with skin the color of paper stopped Dre and Dea, and my blood froze in my veins when I saw the hint of fangs in their mouths. My eyes remained glued to them like white on rice as they dropped presents on the table and went to greet Nedasea.

"Steer clear of the guys that just arrived. They're vamps and can thrall you in a heartbeat." I was glad to see Dre and Dea seemed unaffected.

Dakota sucked in a breath and cursed as I pulled out my phone and texted Noah. We were supposed to have shifter help, but no one had arrived yet. I was supremely glad we had agreed to the arrangement given our latest guests.

Noah's reply was immediate that he and Lucas were on their way and had gotten detained by traffic. That was the one thing I hated about living here. There was always traffic thanks to the tourists that flocked here year-round.

When Nedasea sent the vamps a scowl, I hurried in that direction. I had no idea what I would do, but I didn't want things becoming explosive and destroying our house. "What was that protection spell Kaitlyn mentioned?" I whispered to Dakota as she stayed beside me.

She was breathing heavily as we walked, but didn't ask me to slow down. "The one for sirens is *impedimentum olfactus sanum.*" I recalled Kaitlyn saying we would want to imagine noise-canceling headphones covering our ears so the siren's song could not get past them.

I shook my head. "No. Not that one. The one to protect ourselves. I don't want the vampires to thrall us."

Dakota shot wide eyes in my direction. "What do you mean? Holy shit, I take back what I said a moment ago. What the hell?"

I opened my mouth to reply when I noticed several more guests gliding up the path toward the party. These women reminded me of the way Nedasea moved with fluid grace.

Nedasea was worked up as we got closer and shouted at the newcomers to leave her event immediately. Dreya stepped up along with Dahlia, Phi, and Dea. "What's the problem?"

Neda clenched her jaw and spoke through her teeth. "I didn't invite them. They need to leave."

Dakota and I were panting when we reached them. One of the new women glowered at Nedasea. "You will return home and live as a siren should? We will not allow you to lose your song."

"Fuck you, mom. I'm not going back. I refuse to give up when I'm a couple of hours away from never having to worry about the urge to sing overcoming me again." Nedasea's translucent skin darkened, and she was seething.

Between one second and the next, a melody floated through the air and the tension left my body. I spat the spell Kota had told me a second before and grabbed her hand. "Cast the earplugs!"

One of the siren women jumped over the vamps, who were standing there glassy-eyed, and punched me in the face as she landed in front of me. I stumbled back and reached for my other sisters.

Lia's shirt slipped through my fingers as I ran backward, away from the woman. Thankfully, Dakota nudged the others, and I heard the spell repeated five more times. My attacker had knocked me off-balance. I had to steady myself by grabbing one of the other guests by the arm.

Her glassy eyes vanished and she gasped as she took in the scene. She went vacant when I let her go. Latching on, I focused my intent on giving those at the table closest to me earplugs while also snatching up forks and knives and throwing them at the siren attacking me.

The table's occupants joined in and I was able to get away from the woman only to find my sisters and Nedasea in a battle with the sirens. Lucas and Noah were running from the parking lot and stopped in their tracks, becoming zombie-like.

The party guests started walking in the direction of the river that was half a mile away from the plantation. We had to stop this, but I was at a loss as to how to do that. Our best bet was currently under the influence of the siren's song.

"Give earplugs to Noah and Lucas," I shouted to Lia and Dreya, who were closest to the shifters. I was way too damn far away.

BRENDA TRIM

Dahlia nodded and turned to face Lucas. She was mid-chant when a siren tackled her to the ground. I hadn't noticed the siren woman. The majority of them remained focused on the party guests and keeping them moving away from the house, leaving three to deal with the rest of us.

Lia's hands shot out and broke her fall. Deandra was right there using the skills her kick-boxing coach taught her to plant her left foot in the siren's solar plexus. Phi joined Dea, and they fought the siren while Lia cast earplugs over Lucas and Noah.

Kota conjured a machete and handed it to me, then made one for herself. Steve came running from the back of the property with a baseball bat in hand. He paused when he saw the women involved. Unfortunately, no one was close enough and his eyes turned glassy and he did an about-face to fall into line with the party guests.

A growl rattled my bones, and I looked up in time to see Lucas turn into his grey wolf. Noah was right behind him in shifting. The two wolves pounced on the nearest sirens and clamped their jaws around fragile necks.

Bile rose in my throat as blood spurted around their mouths. The sirens fell to the ground and didn't move. The wolves didn't pause as they worked their way through the sirens.

I went to Nedasea and checked on the siren. "Are you alright?"

With her gaze glued to what Lucas and Noah were doing, she nodded her head. "I'm fine. No! She's mine."

The last part was said to Lucas, who had Neda's mother pinned to the ground. It was clear what Nedasea meant. She wanted to be the one to deal with her mother. Party guests returned as they were released from their thrall.

Lucas leaped from Neda's mom and helped Noah deal with the rest of the sirens. Within seconds, the nearly dozen sirens that had arrived to try and convince Nedasea to return to the fold were no longer a problem.

I admired the siren for not wanting to be part of that life-style. It couldn't have been easy to go against her nature as she had. And to stand firm when they pulled out a last-ditch effort was remarkable.

I winced as I scanned the crowd and noticed the dead bodies. Thankfully, none of the guests were hurt. Most stood around watching as Neda faced off with her mother, who was spitting curses at her daughter.

Nedasea put a hand under the side of her skirt and came back with a palm full of shiny metal. The thin silver blade glinted in the fairy lights we'd strung everywhere. I cried out when Neda swiped the blade across her mother's throat.

A wet gurgling sound left her mother as she fell to her knees, clutching her neck. Sizzling blood seeped between her fingers and flowed down her forearms. Neda bent to get in her mother's face. "You will never hurt another soul with your vile song again. I renounced my ability long ago and now I'm finally free."

With that, Nedasea whooped and circled her finger to Drake. "Let's get this party started!"

Brezok held up two bottles of alcohol. "This calls for a savage freedom!"

Based on the whoops and hollers, the fame demon was talking about a drink. He put on a show as he mixed, poured, and served. Noah and Lucas drug the bodies away while Steve washed away the blood.

Dakota pointed to the mother with her machete. "What about her?"

I watched Nedasea drinking and dancing and knew she wasn't going to do a thing about her mom. Dreya sighed and grabbed Kota's arm. "We are going to make her leave."

The rest of us shared a look, then followed them to the

injured and bleeding woman. We stopped in a v formation behind Dakota and Dreya. Dakota pointed her sword at the siren.

Dreya crossed her arms over her chest. "You are not welcome here. Leave now or forfeit your life."

"Bu...but, where?" Nedasea's mother was shattered. It was a stark contrast to how she looked when she arrived to force her daughter to return home.

Dakota shook the machete. "We don't give a shit. Leave now!"

The woman stumbled as she got to her feet and walked away. I should feel bad about what happened to her, but I didn't. And I refused to ask if the other sirens were dead or alive. They'd come onto our property and planned on killing everyone present to get Nedasea back under their control.

I wrapped my arm around Delphine's shoulders. "Let's get one of those drinks and see if the food needs to be replenished."

"I can't believe they're still going to party after that," Lia murmured.

Brezok extended a tray filled with green drinks in our direction. "Why let shit like that ruin a good party? The night just got started."

I laughed and accepted a cocktail and toasted my sisters for successfully casting our first spell under pressure. We'd just finished our drinks when a good-looking guy approached us.

He lifted a hand in greeting. "I'm Albar. You guys throw an amazing party and have great security in place. Can I book you for an event for my office?" His voice was a bit like boulders rubbing together.

Phi reacted before my mind could process his request. It was the second time that night we had been asked to plan an event. "What kind of event did you have in mind?"

A grin crossed Albar's face. "I'd like to throw a cocktail party as a thank you to everyone for a good quarter. I'm a broker and we made more the last three months than we did the second half of last year."

I nodded my head. "That wouldn't be a problem. We will need to set up a time to go over the theme and what you want us to cover. Also, if there will be mundies present. Certain precautions will need to be taken."

Albar inclined his head. Phi took down the information he shared and reserved the date before he went back to the party. I sighed and watched the guests eat and drink as if nothing had interrupted the fun. "How is this going to work if he will have mundies present? Shit always seems to go sideways these days."

Dahlia shrugged her shoulders. "The magical employees of his must have some kind of glamour charms or they couldn't work that closely with regular humans. Whatever we do, we will have to ask Lucas and Noah for extra protection. We can't risk mundies being exposed."

Phi told us about a call she got from an elf to host a graduation party for her mate. He was graduating from medical school at the end of the semester. She also received a call from a woman who lost her mother and wanted us to plan the second line parade for her. Regardless of the species, beings in the magical world wanted to celebrate the same important life events as mundies.

It seemed funny to me that one society was hidden and separate from another when they had so much in common. Of course, they had even more differences. We straddled the line between the two worlds. We were the only organization that could bring them together safely. I had a feeling between the events and Dahlia's visions we would be busier than we knew how to handle.

. . .

DOWNLOAD the next book in the Twisted Sisters Midlife Maelstrom series, Seances and Second Line Parades HERE! Then turn the page for a preview.

Preorder for the next book in the Mystical Midlife in Maine series, Fae Forged Axes and Chin Waxes! Turn the page for a preview.

EXCERPT FROM SEANCES AND SECOND LINE PARADES BOOK #3

DANIELLE

"I'd feel better if I went in with you guys? There could be ghosts in there." Maliko told Dea as pulled up to the curb outside of the One Stop Shop at City Hall.

"Somehow, I'll manage. My sisters have magic like me, babe. They can help if things go sideways," Dea replied before she leaned over and gave him a kiss.

I loved seeing Deandra happy. She'd come a long way from her troubled teen years. Dea was the last of us to get married a few years ago. She had her first son at seventeen and two more a few years after that.

We watched her struggle for years and couldn't be prouder of the hard work she put in to turn her life around. She met Maliko in the process and the two of them were one of the cutest couples I knew.

Maliko was an islander with a laid-back attitude and a deep soul. He was on the shorter side for a guy, but he was fit which made up for it. Add to that his dark complexion, black hair and dark eyes and he was a good looking guy and he loved our sister deeply. He'd become even more over-protective than usual since our magic was unlocked.

Lia patted Maliko on the shoulder. "We're go into a government establishment for a permit not paying Marie Leveau a visit."

I hide my smirk as we got out of the car. When Maliko discovered we needed to go to the permit office for our latest client and that Dea was coming with us because she was friends with one of the clerks, he'd insisted on driving us.

Maliko waved. "I'll be back to pick you guys up shortly. You want a coconut water, babe?"

Dea smiled at her husband. "Unless you find a margarita where you stop that'll work."

"I'll grab a tall-boy and an energy drink for you guys, as well," Maliko called out before he pulled away from the curb.

Dea laughed and shook her head. "That man, I swear. He's been impossible at times."

Lia adjusted my bag on her shoulder and pulled the folder out. "He's worried about you. You're part of a world that he isn't and when you struggle, there is nothing he can do to help. He's doing what he can."

Dea's powers had been emerging more and more and making it difficult for her to walk the line between the mundie world and the magical one. It was something we'd been working on as much as her busy life allowed. And, Maliko was having just as hard of a time adjusting.

"He's not hurting anyone by driving you around. He still gives you the space you need," I pointed out. She was like the rest of us in that she was fiercely independent yet co-dependent at the same time.

We wanted to be free to do what we wanted while also having each other there to do it with us. To most it likely made no sense, but that's what made us the Six Twisted Sisters. All that mattered were that my sisters' husbands had come to understand and appreciate what we had with each other.

Dea shrugged. "He asks me every few hours if there are any ghosts in the house and he vacillates between anxious, excited, and terrified. It's hard to know he's afraid of the changes."

I placed a hand on Dea's shoulder. "You've always been tuned into everyone's emotions. It's got to be difficult actually knowing how people feel now."

We'd called Kaitlyn when Deandra's symptoms started getting worse. She was the one that confirmed Dea was an empath as well as having some necromancer skills with ghosts and spirits.

We were truly muts of the magical world. So far, we'd shown signs of nearly every magical species out there save for vampires. It had been exciting to see how each of us was developing until Deandra started experiencing all the horrendous emotions of her patients. The focus during magical practice last time had shifted to how to control the input so she could get a handle on things before it drove her crazy.

She snorted. "You have no idea. It's gut wrenching to feel the anger and resentment of those newly diagnosed as terminal. Enough of that. We need to go see Shannon and get our permit for this second line parade. Were you guys able to find a band?"

I happily made the shift. The only second line parade we'd done was the one for Lia's late husband. We hadn't done one for a customer and I was excited to do one without the sadness permeating the process.

Although, I had to admit that it would have been nice if we were planning the parade for a wedding as is typically the case nowadays, but it was still fun to help our client plan the perfect event to honor her mother.

"Phi received confirmation yesterday. It's not the same one we used for Leo. She told me the name. It's here somewhere." Lia opened the folder and flipped through the pages that included the route that we'd planned through the Quarter along with our parade escorts and the name of the brass band we'd arranged.

Dea pulled the door open as we reached the building. "Don't worry about it. You have the application, correct? Because Shannon can't help without that."

I moved around her and entered the office without touching anything. I'd taken to wearing gloves around the house to avoid triggering my magic, but out in public it was harder to explain why I had leather gloves on. Especially in the middle of the hot summer months.

Lia lifted a piece of paper in the air triumphantly but her response was cut off when Dea gasped and froze in place. I moved closer to her and touched her arm. "Are you okay, Dea?"

"There are ghosts everywhere. Can't you see them?" Dea's face had blanched of color.

I scanned the room. The office looked like any government agency with a counter where clerks assisted people and chairs situated in the space on the other side. The information desk as set off to the side along with forms of all kinds. The place was filled with mundies and smelled like despair and boredom, if those emotions had a scent.

I didn't see one ghost which was unusual for New Orleans. We had a rich history and plenty of spirits that have stuck around for centuries. What was crazy was that before stepping foot on Willowberry, I had never seen one before. Our mom and Dea were the only ones that had previously seen one.

When Phoebe unlocked our magic, we gained more than just powers. However, paranormals could only see certain types of spirits lingering on this side. No one had been able to explain to us why Dea could see what others couldn't. That was typically the power of a necromancer. Her having it was part of that mixed breed heritage in our family.

"I don't see a thing," I told her.

Dea 's eyes unfocused as she concentrated on creating an aura around herself that would repel the ghosts. Temperence, the necromancer that Phoebe had freed from Marie Leveau's control, was helping Dea learn skills to deal with this aspect of her magic.

I couldn't see what she was doing but I felt the warmth and tingle of her power as it took effect. A second later Dea put a smile on her face and crossed the lobby to the line of people waiting to be helped.

A middle-aged Hispanic woman stood up from a desk behind the counter and waved at us. Shannon's smile was bright as she gestured to the left where there was a door marked employees only.

We followed Dea and met the woman the second she flung the panel open. "Dea! How are you doing? You've missed the past two girls' night out."

Dea laughed, but it wasn't her usual infectious amusement that made you want to join her. "I've had to work doubles with the nursing shortage. And then there is the plantation. If I'm not at the hospital, I'm at Willowberry."

Shannon sucked in a breath. "That's right. How's that going? I really need to get out there and see the place." She gestured for us to follow her to her desk. I kept my arms folded over my chest with my hands tucked under my armpits.

"It's going better than we expected," I admitted. I left out the fact that most of our customers were magical creatures that would make her crap her pants.

Lia nodded as she took a seat in one of the chairs

Shannon grabbed for us. "We've hired a woman to start running tours during the day and Dre and Steve moved into one of the buildings."

Dea jerked her arm toward her chest making Shannon frown at her. Crap, the spirits must be bothering her. I reached for her then let my hand drop. Being psychometric wasn't all it's cracked up to be. I looked forward to the time I could let my guard down at home. Kaitlyn had assured me that I would eventually become immune to my environment.

I smiled, hoping it didn't look too strained. "Of course, not all of our events are being held at the plantation which is why we are here. We have a client that wants a second line for her mom who recently passed but it's less than two weeks away."

Shannon winced as she turned off her screen saver. "That could be a problem. The city is careful about the timing of these and the routes taken."

"You know we can't bring you an easy request," Dea laughed.

Shannon rolled her eyes then accepted the papers from Lia. "Let's see what we can do. It's possible you will need to move the event. I know it isn't ideal but if your client is set on have a second line, it might be necessary."

I moved my seat closer to Dea as she batted at something to the side of her chair. Shannon was busy typing on her computer. I nudged Lia and jerked my head in Dea's direction then back at Shannon.

Lia's eyes flared before she nodded. She leaned forward and grabbed a frame from the desk, keeping her body angled so she hid Dea from view. "Is this Frankie now? Man, he's gotten so big. I remember when he was just a little guy running around the park."

Shannon stopped typing to smile. "Can you believe he's

thirteen now? He actually made me breakfast Sunday morning and brought it to me on a tray. The pancakes were good, too."

"You're doing something right, then," Lia replied. "My kids are all too busy to stop and think about making mom a bowl of cereal let alone pancakes. Although, Eli does make a mean grilled cheese sandwich."

I made an appreciative noise thinking about the sandwich Lia's son had made me a few weeks ago right before we moved into the plantation. "They are delicious. He adds cheese to the outside too and cooks it until it crunchy so you have that layer plus the gooey enter. Oh, and then there's the hint of truffle salt."

Shannon and Lia talked cheese while Shannon went back to work. I turned and checked on Dea. She was sitting there with her hands clenched into fists. Sweat dotted her brow and her mouth was pinched.

Whatever was happening, it was triggering Dea's magic and draining her. None of us were practiced enough to shut it down at home during magical practice. Forget about the stress of being in a public place where one of your close friends was helping you. The situation was the perfect storm.

Shannon's voice made my head turn in her direction. "You're in luck. Your route and day are free. I am sliding you into the slot and granting your permit now."

"Thank God," Dea replied. "Losing your mom is tough enough."

Shannon gave Dea the smile people got when you lost a loved one. It displayed their unease more than sympathy for what you were going through. It screamed *I have no idea what to say to you right now.*

Cold air suddenly surrounded me making me shiver. It would have been perfect if I was having one of the never-ending hot flashes. Lia did the same thing and glanced around as surreptitiously as possible.

"There goes the air conditioner again. I swear they need another HVAC guy. The temperature shouldn't fluctuate this much," Shannon observed as she typed several more things then pressed a button.

The whir of the printer behind her started up a second later before it spit out several pages. Shannon picked them up and handed them over. I kept my hands tucked in my lap while Lia accepted them and tucked them into the folder.

Dea stood up when Shannon did and hugged her. "Thanks, girl. We owe you one."

Shannon chuckled. "You can repay me by joining us for taco Tuesday next week. Oh, and tell your clients they can't cut it so close next time."

"I'll be there," Dea promised her friend as she walked us to the door. I shivered as the cold

Deandra grabbed my arm and tugged me to the bathroom to the right of the entrance. Lia moved ahead of us and pushed the door open. I bent to check under the stall doors to see if anyone was in there.

I shook my head to let them know there was still someone in one of the stalls. I leaned against the wall next to the sink where Dea washed her hands. Lia hovered nearby as she stuffed the folder back inside her bag.

"Hold this for me, sestra," Lia said to Dea.

Dea finished drying her hands then took the strap while Dahlia entered a stall. While Lia relieved herself the other woman finished up, washed her hands and left. Dea was scowling at thin air by the time Lia came out.

Dea paced back and forth. "What will it take for you to leave me alone? I'm not some ghost whisperer here to do your bidding. I wish you'd just freaking leave me alone."

Dahlia met my gaze in the mirror as she washed her

hands. I lifted one shoulder but remained silent. Dea stopped, shook her head and thrust her hands on her hips. "I'm not going to act as your spokesperson with your sister. I'm sorry you're dead, but there is nothing I can do for you."

I was surprised to hear our happy sister sounds irritated and upset. Dea laughed more often than not and rarely got testy with people. This ghost thing really was pushing her to the edge of her sanity.

The color drained from Dea's face and her hand flew to her mouth. "How are you bound together? I don't understand."

I straightened off the wall. "What is it?"

Dea waved her arm through the air. "Giselle here says that she needs help contacting her twin sister, Georgette, because the two of them are bound together."

Lia's forehead furrowed. "How will contacting her help? It'll only cause any grief she's lived with to resurface. That will make it harder to learn to cope without her sister."

Dea wrapped her arms around her torso. "She says her sister will lose her mind to madness unless I help them."

This had become our life lately. We'd encounter any number of supernatural events while out trying to do normal mundane things, like obtain a permit for a parade. Just like the vision Dahlia had been hit with a couple weeks ago about a dead woman being dumped on Canal Street, this request from a ghost came out of the blue.

I pinched the bridge of my nose. "I suppose this isn't something we can ignore. So, how do we help her? Does she know where to find her sister?"

The door opened making all three of us jump out of our skin. The woman that had come stopped and took a step back. "Is, uh, everything alright in here?"

I smiled at her and gestured to Dea who was still pale and shaken. "We're great. My sister here was just telling us the ghost story about what this place was used for and it shook us."

The woman's eyes went wide and she looked around. "You must be some story teller. What was it used for? I haven't heard anything about this building."

Deandra rubbed her hands theatrically. "It wasn't the office, but the location. Rumor has it this was the site of a bloody battle between the English and the French. I don't know how true it is, but my friend said hundreds of soldiers died here and still haunt the location. But she must be wrong. You don't see any ghosts, do you?"

My heart was racing and my mind pondered the accuracy of Dea's story. Battles had been fought all over our fair city at one point or another, so the chance were high that she was telling the truth.

I had never seen the ghost of a soldier, and from her description, it seemed like perhaps she had. It made me wonder if their wounds were visible after they died and came back a ghost.

The woman shook her head. "Not one. Some of the stories in this city are outrageous. Don't believe half of what you hear. It's great for tourism but that's about it."

Lia and I laughed as the lady went into one of the stalls. Lia, who was standing next to the sink, turned on the faucet and proceeded to wash her hands. She took her time scrubbing them until after the woman left.

Lia shifted her gaze to Dea with pursed lips. "Was your story true? And how can we find this sister fast? We need to get the hell out of here before someone else comes in."

Dea blew out a breath. "It's difficult to communicate with ghosts. Giselle hasn't managed to tell me more than their first names."

My shoulders sagged and I moved to leave. "We will have

to deal with this later. Tell her we will come back." The evil side of me silently added, or not.

"She's not happy about that idea," Dea replied.

I clenched my jaw shut. "Explain to her this isn't the place to get into this with her. If she persists, she could get us committed."

"She heard you and said she will come with us." Dea moved around me to open the door. The panel slammed into the wall as she yanked it open.

Lia gasped and glanced around. "She can't do that."

We were close to the exit, so it didn't take us long before we were outside on the sidewalk. Dea searched for Maliko. "I don't think she cares about what she can and can't do, Lia. Her spirit is following me. Shit, we need to do something. You can't come home with me, Giselle. Maliko will rethink how much he loves me if I start brings ghosts home like lost dogs."

My heart squeezed hearing the frantic worry in my sister's voice. "We can bring her back to Willowberry. There are plenty of places outside the main house where she can haunt."

Deandra waved at Maliko who was parked a few feet in front of us at the curb. "I owe you both big time. You're saving me a huge headache."

I pulled my gloves out and slipped them on so I didn't catch a glimpse of something in Maliko's car. The last thing I needed was to add to the headache blooming behind my eyes. "Tell her to follow us to the plantation."

I thanked Maliko for the tall boy he'd picked me up and considered taking a swig of Dea's margarita. This day had already been eventful and it was still early.

GLOSSARY OF SIX TWISTED
SISTERS & THEIR HUSBANDS

*D*reya – Her nickname is Dre and she is the oldest sister of the Six Twisted Sisters. She is also the third of the Smith children. Her power is telekinesis.

Dakota – Her nickname is Kota and she is the second oldest sister of the Six Twisted Sisters. She is also the fourth child of the Smith children. Her Frenchies are named: Daisy, Willow and Scout and her power is materialization.

Dahlia – Her nickname is Lia and she is the third oldest sister of the Six Twisted Sisters. She is also the sixth child of the Smith Children, Her Frenchies are named: Oscar and Zoe and her power is scent induced premonitions.

Danielle – Her nickname is Dani and she is the fourth oldest sister of the Six Twisted Sisters. She is also the seventh child of the Smith children. Her Frenchie is named Frida and her power is psychometry.

Deandra – Her nickname is Dea and she is the fifth oldest sister of the Six Twisted Sisters. She is also the ninth child of the Smith children. Her powers are empathy and the ability to see spirits on every plane.

Delphine – Her nickname is Phi and she is the sixth

oldest sister of the Six Twisted Sisters. She is also the youngest child; of the Smith children. She has the power to freeze objects.

Steve – Dreya's Husband

Jeff – Dakota's Husband

Leo – Dahlia's Late Husband

Hugo – Danielle's Second Husband

Mike – Danielle's First Husband

Maleko – Deandra's Husband

Tucker – Delphine's Husband

GLOSSARY OF SMITH FAMILY

Dean – Oldest brother and oldest child
   Dawson – Second oldest brother and second child
   Dominic – Third oldest brother and fifth child
   Dagen – Youngest brother and eighth child
   Sawyer – Dreya & Steve's oldest son
   Spencer - Dreya & Steve's second son
   Sean - Dreya & Steve's third son
   Scarlett - Dreya & Steve's daughter and youngest child
   Braxton – Jeff and Dakota's son and youngest child
   Kora - Jeff and Dakota's third daughter and third child
   Annabelle - Jeff and Dakota's first daughter and oldest
child
   Mia - Jeff and Dakota's second daughter and second child
   Tegan – Dahlia & Leo's youngest daughter and last child
   Eli – Dahlia & Leo's son and second child
   Mackenna - Dahlia & Leo's oldest daughter and oldest
child
   Ashton – Danielle & Mike's son, one of the twins
   Ava - Danielle & Mike's second daughter, one of the
twins

Genevive - Danielle & Mike's oldest daughter and oldest child

Mason – Deandra & Maleko's oldest son

Maverick - Deandra & Maleko's second son

Mateo - Deandra & Maleko's third son

Matiu - Deandra & Maleko's youngest son

Justin – Delphine & Tucker's son and youngest child

Rachel - Delphine & Tucker's daughter and oldest child

Stephanie – Dagen's wife

Rory – Dagen & Stephanie's oldest son and oldest child

Addilyn - Dagen & Stephanie's daughter and youngest child

Zak - Dagen & Stephanie's second son and second child

Tracy – Dominic's wife

Tom – Dominic & Tracy's oldest son and oldest child

Terrance - Dominic & Tracy's youngest son and youngest child

Madeline - Dominic & Tracy's oldest daughter and second child

Maisy - Dominic & Tracy's second daughter and third child

Brianna – Dawson's ex-wife

Cassandra – Dawson & Brianna's oldest daughter and oldest child

Lilly - Dawson & Brianna's second daughter and second child; one of twins

Celeste - Dawson & Brianna's third daughter and second child; one of twins

Liam - Dawson & Brianna's son and youngest child

Nancy – Dean's ex-wife

Gracie – Dean & Nancy's youngest daughter and youngest child

Nicole – Dean and Nancy's oldest daughter and oldest child

AUTHORS' NOTE

Reviews are like hugs. Sometimes awkward. Always welcome! It would mean the world to me if you can take five minutes and let others know how much you enjoyed my work.

Don't forget to visit my website: www.brendatrim.com and sign up for my newsletter, which is jam-packed with exciting news and monthly giveaways. Also, be sure to visit and like my Facebook page https://www.facebook.com/AuthorBrendaTrim to see my daily posts.

Never allow waiting to become a habit. Live your dreams and take risks. Life is happening now.

DREAM BIG!

XOXO,

Brenda

ALSO BY BRENDA TRIM

The Dark Warrior Alliance

Dream Warrior (Dark Warrior Alliance, Book 1)

Mystik Warrior (Dark Warrior Alliance, Book 2)

Pema's Storm (Dark Warrior Alliance, Book 3)

Isis' Betrayal (Dark Warrior Alliance, Book 4)

Deviant Warrior (Dark Warrior Alliance, Book 5)

Suvi's Revenge (Dark Warrior Alliance, Book 6)

Mistletoe & Mayhem (Dark Warrior Alliance, Novella)

Scarred Warrior (Dark Warrior Alliance, Book 7)

Heat in the Bayou (Dark Warrior Alliance, Novella, Book 7.5)

Hellbound Warrior (Dark Warrior Alliance, Book 8)

Isobel (Dark Warrior Alliance, Book 9)

Rogue Warrior (Dark Warrior Alliance, Book 10)

Shattered Warrior (Dark Warrior Alliance, Book 11)

King of Khoth (Dark Warrior Alliance, Book 12)

Ice Warrior (Dark Warrior Alliance, Book 13)

Fire Warrior (Dark Warrior Alliance, Book 14)

Ramiel (Dark Warrior Alliance, Book 15)

Rivaled Warrior (Dark Warrior Alliance, Book 16)

Dragon Knight of Khoth (Dark Warrior Alliance, Book 17)

Ayil (Dark Warrior Alliance, Book 18)

Guild Master (Dark Alliance Book 19)

Maven Warrior (Dark Alliance Book 20)

Sentinel of Khoth (Dark Alliance Book 21)

Araton (Dark Warrior Alliance Book 22)

Cambion Lord (Dark Warrior Alliance Book 23)

Omega (Dark Warrior Alliance Book 24)

Dragon Lothario of Khoth (Dark Warrior Alliance Book 25)

Dark Warrior Alliance Boxsets:

Dark Warrior Alliance Boxset Books 1-4

Dark Warrior Alliance Boxset Books 5-8

Dark Warrior Alliance Boxset Books 9-12

Dark Warrior Alliance Boxset Books 13-16

Dark Warrior Alliance Boxset Books 17-20

Hollow Rock Shifters:

Captivity, Hollow Rock Shifters Book 1

Safe Haven, Hollow Rock Shifters Book 2

Alpha, Hollow Rock Shifters Book 3

Ravin, Hollow Rock Shifters Book 4

Impeached, Hollow Rock Shifters Book 5

Anarchy, Hollow Rock Shifters Book 6

Allies, Hollow Rock Shifters Book 7

Sovereignty, Hollow Rock Shifters Book 8

Midlife Witchery:

Magical New Beginnings Book 1

Mind Over Magical Matters

Magical Twist

My Magical Life to Live

Forged in Magical Fire

Like a Fine Magical Wine

Magical Yule Tidings

Magical Complications

Magical Delivery

Magical Moxie

Mystical Midlife in Maine

Magical Makeover

Laugh Lines & Lost Things

Hellmouths & Hot Flashes

Holiday with Hades

Saggy But Witty in Crescent City

Nasty Curses & Big Purses

Fae Forged Axes & Chin Waxes

Demonic Stones & Creaky Bones

Twisted Sisters' Midlife Maelstrom

Packing Serious Magical Mojo

Cadaver on Canal Street

Seances & Second Line Parades

French Quarter Fae

Bramble's Edge Academy:

Unearthing the Fae King

Masking the Fae King

Revealing the Fae King

Midnight Doms:

Her Vampire Bad Boy

Her Vampire Suspect

All Souls Night

Printed in Great Britain
by Amazon

48241025R00138